AN IMPRINT OF EVIL AND OTHER HAUNTINGS

An Imprint of Evil and Other Hauntings

STEPHEN TALLEVI

CONTENTS

To my family

First published by Stephen Tallevi 2026

This novel is entirely a work of fiction. The names,
characters and incidents portrayed in it are the
work of the author's imagination. Any resemblance
to actual persons, living or dead, events or localities
is entirely coincidental.

Stephen Tallevi asserts the moral right to be identified as the author of this work.

First edition

Certain houses, like certain persons, manage somehow to proclaim at once their character for evil.

—The Empty House (Algernon Blackwood)

LOVE IS BLIND

Manchester, 1831

"Let's stop here for a moment. So wonderful to feel the warmth of the sun on my face after enduring a week of dreary rain. Tell me, are there any clouds in the sky?"

"Not a one, my dear Mary. A brilliant shade of blue as far as the eye can see."

"Lovely. We are free to enjoy our walk today without fear of rain."

She held out her hand, which Henry accepted, slipping her arm through his as they continued their stroll down the gravel path that meandered through the city's botanical garden.

"I will miss you, my dear Henry," Mary remarked, a hint of concern evident in her tone. "Three months is a long time. Have they told you anything more about your mission?"

"There have been a number of skirmishes recently in the Gold Coast colony involving the Ashanti army. British officials believe war is inevitable unless we swiftly put a stop to their activities. Our regiment is being sent to help quell the unrest. Not a dangerous mission, you can rest assured that I will return."

"Thank you for reassuring me. I don't know how I would manage without my best friend by my side."

Henry glanced in her direction and let out a light laugh. "My dear Mary, it is you that looks after me."

She smiled and gave his arm a slight squeeze. "Will you pick me a flower?"

"Certainly, but I do not think the gardeners would be all too pleased if they saw me doing so."

He left her side for a minute before returning with a pink, bell-shaped flower which he placed in her hand. Gently, she traced her fingers over the flower's petals before inhaling its fragrance.

"Why, it's a flower from an azalea shrub. I may be blind, but I have an excellent sense of smell. Is it pink?"

"Yes, a soft shade of pink that perfectly complements the colour of your cheeks."

"Henry, you're such a charmer!" she said with obvious delight. "I feel myself blushing. Now I'll need to exchange the pink flower for a red one!"

They continued their leisurely stroll for the better part of an hour before returning to Mary's residence, a quaint, two-bedroom cottage situated across the extensive gardens at the rear of the main house. Her father had the place constructed in time for her twentieth birthday, knowing that it would grant her the ability to live more independently.

"You will stay and dine with us this afternoon. I told Sarah you would."

"I would be delighted. I can smell Sarah's delicious cooking from here. I'm so glad...." Henry hesitated, then asked, "Are we eating outdoors?"

"What...are you glad of, Henry?" Mary inquired gently.

"I was going to say that I'm very grateful that Sarah is in your life. I will be more at ease knowing she is by your side while I am away."

"Yes, she is a remarkable woman. I cannot begin to imagine how different my life would be without her."

Sarah entered Mary's life when she was a child of five. Sir Thomas, Mary's father, owned a sizable sugar estate in the West Indies. He decided to move the family from Manchester to their great plantation home in Jamaica at the turn of the century. The decision was an unfortunate one. Mary's mother succumbed to Cholera but a few weeks following their arrival. Sarah, who worked as a domestic servant at the home, took on the duty of nanny. At first, Mary was somewhat fearful of this tall woman with smooth dark skin, but she soon found herself drawn to her gentle and caring manner. Within a few weeks, Mary felt as close to Sarah as she had been to her own mother. As for Sir Thomas, he was relieved to see his child happy and playful so soon after his wife's passing, and so decided it would do no harm to remain at the estate for a few more months, possibly a year at most. But this was not to be.

One afternoon, Sarah and Mary were returning from a picnic they enjoyed beneath a sprawling Jacaranda tree situated on the grounds of the estate. The day had darkened suddenly with a threatening sky, and as they approached the manor, a tremendous crash of thunder resounded overhead. A delivery wagon was just pulling away from the side of the house at that moment, the sound of thunder causing the horses to bolt towards Sarah and Mary. Sarah had just time to pull Mary from the path of the charging beasts, but a wooden crate tumbled off the wagon when it hit a protruding stone and fell upon the poor child.

That evening, the local doctor announced that Mary had lapsed into a coma and was unlikely to recover after sustaining such a blow to the head. Sir Thomas summoned the clergyman that same night, and the following morning had a grave prepared next to her mother's.

Sarah, however, was not prepared to accept the doctor's assessment. "*This child will not die,*" she told the doctor with such conviction that, for a moment, he questioned his medical judgment. "I...hope you are right," he faltered. "To lose a wife and child in such a short span of time would be a great tragedy."

Day and night, Sarah remained by the child's side. At first, Sir Thomas felt uneasy by the woman's constant vigil. He could hear her praying...or chanting...when he stopped to listen from the hallway on his way to bed. But the feeling of unease soon changed into one of gratitude as the child began to show signs of regaining consciousness. By the fifth day of recovery, he walked into Mary's room to find his daughter resting her head on Sarah's shoulder, her small hand securely holding onto Sarah's.

"God in heaven," he said in amazement, "my child is awake…"

Nodding her head, Sarah replied, "She is awake, Master Thomas, but her vision is no more. The child is blind…"

They returned to Manchester that same year. There was never any question that Sarah would accompany the family as the child's caregiver. It was during the return voyage that Sir Thomas made the acquaintance of Sir Reginald and Lady Agnes, who had a six-year old son named Henry. Under Sarah's subtle guidance, the two youngsters became inseparable companions during the voyage, a friendship that endures to this day.

"That was a most delicious meal, Sarah. I'm sure I won't have another like it for several months."

Sarah acknowledged Henry's compliment with a slight nod before turning to Mary to say, "I will retire to my room now, Mary, as I'm sure you and Henry have a lot to discuss."

"Thank you, Sarah," Mary said with a smile. "We shall only be an hour together, as Henry has an early departure tomorrow. But before you go, can you hand me my knitting, it's in the sewing basket" Sarah did so, then left the room.

"What is that you are knitting?" inquired Henry.

"A scarf for you. I understand the evenings in West Africa can get quite chilly this time of year."

"Chilly? In May?" said Henry incredulously. "On the contrary, my dear woman. It's quite hot. Besides..." he went on in a concerned tone, "the colour..."

"What about the colour? It's a lovely shade of violet, I'm told. It will compliment your uniform perfectly." She could not quite disguise the playfulness in her voice as she said this.

"You rascal, you're playing with me!"

"I'm so...sorry...Henry," she replied with laughter. "But you must admit, the image of you marching into battle wearing this knitted scarf is...well, it's just..." She did not finish her sentence as she placed her hand over her mouth to stifle her laughter.

Henry laughed aloud. "I have to confess," he added, "the image is an amusing one. I can picture the expression on the men's faces as I lead them into battle, my scarf billowing in the breeze while sweat drips from my brow! But tell me honestly, who is the scarf for?"

"I've knitted several, this is the last. It's for the church bazaar taking place in a couple of weeks."

Henry got up from his seat and went over to her, bending down to kiss her forehead lightly. "You're a good soul, Mary. Take good care of yourself while I'm gone."

"I will. And may God watch over you and your men."

"Mary! Come quick!" called out Sarah, catching her breath as she entered the cottage.

"What is it? What's happened?"

"I've just come back from the post office. I have a letter from Henry."

"Oh, thank God! I was beginning to worry that something had happened to him. We've heard nothing from him for six weeks. Quickly now, read it to me."

They sat side by side on the sofa as Sarah tore the letter open and read the following:

Dear Mary,

Sorry for the delay in writing to you, but rest assured that all is well with me. There have been a few skirmishes with the enemy but we beat them back quite decisively. Not a single man lost in our company! The Lieutenant believes we should be home in four, perhaps six weeks tops.

And now for the exciting news. I'm-

Sarah stopped reading aloud as she perused the rest of the letter.

"Why have you stopped, Sarah? Don't keep me in suspense, tell me the exciting news."

Sarah lifted her gaze from the letter and said uneasily, "Henry...he's engaged to be married."

"Engaged..." Mary said under her breath in disbelief. And then tears filled her eyes.

"My dear Mary, please don't cry. I can't believe the news myself. You are the–"

"It's alright, Sarah," Mary broke in, "It was foolish of me to ever think Henry would consider me more than a friend. No one in their right mind would marry a blind woman. He deserves more and I'm glad he has found her." She wiped the tears from her cheeks and gave a long sigh. "There, all better. I think I would like to go for a walk, if you're up to accompanying me."

"Of course, Mary. I'll get our shawls."

The following morning, Sarah announced, "Mary, Lady Audrey is her to see you,"

"Lady Audrey? This is quite a surprise. Please show her in, Sarah."

Mary sat up from the sofa as she heard Lady Audrey enter the room. "Mary, my dear, you are looking as beautiful as ever."

"Lady Audrey, what a delightful surprise! Thank you for the kind words. What do I owe the pleasure of this visit?"

"Sir David had some business to discuss with your father. I decided to come along to pay you a visit. It's been too long since we last spoke. How have you been, my dear?"

"Quite well, thank you. But please come and take a seat next to me. Sarah will prepare us some tea."

Once tea had been served, Lady Audrey inquired, "I presume you've heard that Henry is getting married?"

"Yes, we received a letter from him yesterday in which he told us the good news. I'm very happy for him."

"Such a wonderful man, and the bride-to-be is a lovely girl as well."

"You know her?" Mary asked in surprise.

"Why of course I know Alice. Her father, Sir Richard, and my husband were in the army together. We know the Haywards very well. Sir Richard is now a high ranking official within the Gold Coast administration. I believe Sir Richard met Henry at a military function and took an immediate liking to the boy. He arranged to have him meet his daughter at a luncheon the following day. I daresay the two felt a mutual attraction from the very beginning, and it wasn't long after that Henry proposed to her."

"I see, it was love at first sight," Mary reflected, then asked, "Would it be possible for you to describe Alice to me, if it's not too much trouble?"

"No trouble at all. In several ways she bears a resemblance to you. A lovely round face with perky cheeks and a delicate button nose. Her eyes are brown in colour, a slightly darker shade than yours, and she has full, heart-shaped lips. As for her hair, I would describe it as a unique blend of dark brown with auburn tones. There's not much more I can say, except that she is an inch or two taller than you, and has a lovely physique like yours. I hope that was helpful."

"Very much so. I have no trouble envisioning her in my mind's eye. Thank you ever so much, Lady Audrey."

"Think nothing of it, my dear. Now, enough about Alice, tell me about yourself. What have you been up to lately? I understand you're helping out with the church bazaar this year."

On August thirtieth, Henry returned home. His fiancée, Alice, followed two days later, having spent three weeks in Paris visiting relations. Arrangements were made to visit Mary shortly thereafter for afternoon tea.

"Dear Mary, how wonderful to see you again after all these months. You look wonderful!" Henry took Mary's outstretched hands before leaning forward to kiss her lightly on the cheek she presented to him.

"It's wonderful to have you back, Henry," she said with a warm smile before turning her attention to his right, where she knew Alice would be standing next to him. "Now, be a gentleman and introduce me to your fiancée."

"With pleasure. Mary," he cleared his throat and spoke with an official tone, "Mary, it is my honour to introduce to you my fiancée, Alice."

It's lovely to meet you, Alice." Mary held out her hand and bowed her head slightly when it was accepted by Alice.

"The pleasure is mine, I assure you. Henry has spoken so often about you that I feel as though we've been acquainted for quite some time."

"That is very kind of you, Henry. Let's make our way to the patio where scones and tea are set out for us. You can tell me how the two of you met and I'm anxious to learn more about you, dear Alice. You must be a very special woman to have won Henry's affection so quickly."

Tea was a pleasant affair, with Henry sharing several humourous tales from his recent service abroad. Alice recounted how they met, and detailed some of the challenges of spending time in such a hot region. Mary mentioned Lady Audrey's recent visit, and how she spoke fondly of Alice and highlighted her beauty.

"Alice," continued Mary, "I have a request and would not at all be offended if you denied it."

"I don't see why I would. What is it I can help with?" replied Alice.

"I would like to trace the contour of your face with my hands. Lady Audrey did a wonderful job of describing your features to me, but I don't have a face to place them in!"

"Why of course, Mary. Put out your hands and I'll place them under my chin."

Mary did so and soon felt Alice's delicate skin on her fingertips. Gently, she traced her fingers along the contours of Alice's face, pausing to touch her cheekbones before continuing to her hairline. As Mary withdrew her hands, Alice flinched slightly.

"I'm so sorry, Alice. I felt my ring catch on your hair as I was pulling my hand away. I hope I didn't startle you."

"Not at all. I hope you now have a better idea of what I look like."

"I certainly do. You're very beautiful, Alice. The two of you must make a handsome couple. You have my best wishes for a happy life together."

The wedding took place on the third weekend of September, followed by a week-long bridal tour in Paris, where many of Alice's relatives resided. The couple returned to England and spent a fortnight at the Blackpool Seaside Resort before returning home to Manchester. It was then that Alice showed the first signs of fatigue.

"I don't know what's gotten over me, Henry, but I feel quite drained. Also, I am experiencing a bit of pain in my chest. Perhaps it would be prudent if you summoned Dr. Hughes. All that traveling and rich food may have been too much for me."

While Dr. Hughes found Alice in good physical health, he expressed concern over her symptoms of chest pain and fatigue. "I want you to get plenty of rest the next couple of days, Alice, and have light meals, Herring or Haddock, fruits and vegetables. I'll be back tomorrow to see how you're doing."

Alice did not show any sign of improvement the following day. By week's end, her chest pains had intensified to such an extent that the doctor administered morphia for the pain. Sir Richard had a specialist arrive from London to examine his daughter, but he too could not diagnose the cause of her illness.

"I'm afraid, Sir Richard, that I do not know what afflicts your daughter. She is far too young to be suffering from *angina pectoris*. Besides, she was in excellent health but a few days ago. I know of no heart condition that can cause such suffering in such a short period of time. It pains me to say this, but in my professional opinion, your daughter has but a short time to live."

Alice passed away the following day, clutching at her heart and a horrible expression of agony etched into her once beautiful face. Following the burial, Sarah and Mary were the last to depart. Henry walked over to the women who expressed their heartfelt sympathies. He took Mary's hands and, with a heavy heart, remarked, "She so wanted to be your friend, Mary."

"I'm sorry it was not meant to be, Henry. May her soul rest in peace. I'm always here for you if you need me."

The following day, while Mary was inserting freshly cut flowers into a vase, Sarah entered the room and asked, "Where is the doll, Mary?"

Mary slowly set aside the flower she was holding, and turning towards her, said, "So, you know."

"My dear child, how could I not know? Was it not I who recounted all those stories to you about my ancestors? At first, I told you the voodoo tales as if they were ghost stories, like the ones we read on Christmas Eve. But as you grew older, you started asking for more details, and then it dawned on me that you knew enough to actually perform some of the rituals, to carry out the dark and deadly effigy magic of my ancestors."

There was a moment of silence before Mary asked uneasily, "What do you plan to do now?"

"Do? Why nothing, my dear child. I feel a great sense of pride in knowing I had a helping hand in this event. It was terrible for that wicked woman to take Henry away from you. And to think she wanted to be your friend!"

"Yes, wicked she was," agreed Mary, then added, "The doll is in the sewing basket, beneath the blanket I'm knitting."

Sarah made her way over to the basket and removed the object from its hiding spot. She held a five-inch effigy molded in wax. "Extraordinary..." she murmured in awe, "to mold such details without vision—the face is that of Alice herself. Your talent is truly remarkable. But the figure must possess a personal object from the victim. I do not see one."

"The bracelet. It's made from one of her hairs, wound tightly around the wrist. A strand 'accidentally' caught on my ring under the pretense of examining her face."

Sarah smiled. "You are a clever one, my dear Mary," she said admiringly. "It's a shame the figure must be burned."

"Will you do it for me, Sarah?"

"Of course." She walked over to the wood-burning stove, removed the large knitting needle that pierced the chest of the voodoo doll, then tossed the waxen figure into the flames. She stood there, watching the beautiful face of Alice melt, before asking, "Now that that's taken care of, what do you plan to do next?"

"I always enjoyed the love stories you told me. The ones where a love spell was used to attract a man to fall in love with a woman...forever."

"A love potion. Yes...I believe I can help you with that. There are some lovely herbs growing in the garden that I want you to become familiar with, before the frost settles in."

"Thank you, Sarah," and with a mischievous smile, Mary added, "I can think of no better way to keep my eye on Henry than by being his loving wife."

With an approving nod, Sarah walked over to Mary, took her arm in hers, and led her out to the garden.

IDOL OF THE DEEP

Florida Keys, 1964

"How long has he been under?" I asked, looking overboard at the serene, turquoise water of the Florida Keys.

"About forty minutes," replied Jennifer. "He shouldn't be much longer."

"Always pushing it to the limit. Perhaps he's found a nice stash of gold this time."

She gave me a look that clearly conveyed "as if..." before adding, "That's my big brother, always the optimist."

"Of course I am—we all are or we wouldn't be spending our summer searching for sunken treasure."

"Not me, I'm here to enjoy the sunshine and work on my tan."

I shot my sister the same look she gave me moments ago. She couldn't help but chuckle.

A stream of bubbles reached the water's surface, soon followed by a diver in scuba gear.

"Are we rich?" Jennifer shouted down to Rob.

He lifted his mask before holding up a mesh bag containing a few objects while signaling a thumbs down with his other hand.

"At least he found something this time around," I murmured.

There were five of us on this treasure hunting expedition. We had planned this adventure since our high school days, and it finally became a reality after completing our sophomore year in college, all thanks to Michael, or more precisely, Michael's dad. He had purchased a 34-foot power cruiser the year before, a real beauty, boasting a fiberglass hull, powerful twin engines, and a decent sized pilothouse that could comfortably accommodate the lot of us when it was raining. He christened it *The Osprey*, and agreed to lend it to us for a month in return for twenty percent of the value of all our findings. As he didn't believe we would find any treasure, he told us we were getting the deal of a lifetime. As he put it, 'twenty percent of nothing is nothing.'

Let's hope the old guy's wrong, I reflected as I went over the conversation in my mind.

Rob had made his way onto the deck, and Jennifer was helping him remove his gear when I heard my name being called. I turned to see Michael leaning his head around the doorway of the pilothouse. "Can you spare a minute?" he said in a serious tone, "I think we've picked up a distress signal on the radio."

When I stepped into the cabin, I found John by the radio, jotting something down along the border of a map. Michael was beside him, his head tilted, trying to read what John had written down.

"What's up?" I asked, as I made my way over to the two of them.

"We received an SOS a couple of minutes ago," answered Michael, "John managed to record the coordinates they were transmitting before everything went silent."

"Give me a minute and I'll plot them on the map," volunteered John.

Rob and Jennifer walked in at this point, Rob holding a small mesh bag that was still dripping water. The smile on his face faded when he saw the expression on ours.

"What's going on?" he asked.

"We picked up an SOS," answered Michael, "John's just plotting the coordinates now."

A moment later John turned to face us, holding the map out in front of him. We gathered around to take a look as he explained, "I've marked the spot with an 'X'. I'd estimate it's an hour and a half southwest of our current position."

"Smack in the middle of nowhere," Jennifer observed. "Do we have enough fuel to get there and back?"

"Plenty," replied John.

"Then I think we should head out without delay," I suggested. "Any objections?"

None were put forth.

We set sail and decided to lunch in the pilothouse so that we were sheltered from the intense heat of the midday sun. "Since we've got over an hour to kill," I remarked after glancing at my wristwatch, "why don't we take inventory of this morning's dive?"

"Finally, someone's interested in my hard work," lamented Rob, as he removed the mesh bag from his pocket.

A wooden bench runs the length of one side of the cabin. I got up from my spot and motioned for Rob to empty the contents of the bag there. John remained at the helm, steering the boat, while the rest of us looked on as Rob laid out the few artifacts he had collected.

"The good news is we found silver. The bad news is we found very little of it. We have here four sliver coins that appear to be Spanish Reales, probably fifteenth century. They're heavily worn, and heaven knows which Spanish galleon they originated from. Because of this, I'd guess they're worth a couple of hundred dollars at most."

"That's not bad," Jennifer said encouragingly, "we've only been at it a few days. I'm sure we'll find more when we return. But what's that black object next to the bag—it looks like some kind of grotesque figure."

"That's precisely what it is," Rob replied, holding up the effigy for all to see.

It was about an inch and a half in length, carved in black stone, polished to a high luster. The head was disproportionately large for the body. Its mouth was wide open, as if yelling at us. I could make out the design of a shell necklace that hung low, ending just above two stubby legs. It had a primitive look about it, as if it were carved centuries ago by some tribe on a now forgotten island. It filled me with a kind of primordial fear.

"This little guy is my new lucky charm," Rob continued. "When we get back, he's going to show me where the rest of the silver stash is hidden."

"Looks like a primitive idol. Maybe he's more valuable than the coins," I ventured.

"That hadn't occurred to me," Rob said slowly. "We'll need to have it appraised along with the silver. Our little friend just might be worth a pretty penny to a museum or private collector. Who knows, he may prove to be the best find of this entire expedition."

Fifteen minutes outside of our destination, I started to scan the horizon with my binoculars. I saw nothing in the way of a boat or ship, but a thin, dark line on the horizon caught my attention.

I don't believe it, I said as I lowered my binoculars. After a moment, I shouted for the others to join me.

"Here," I said, handing the glasses to Rob, "scan the horizon and tell me what you see."

I watched as he carefully started to survey the horizon before suddenly focusing on a spot directly ahead of us. He slowly lowered the binoculars and turned to face me with a puzzled expression on his face. "If I had to guess, I'd say that shadowy line in the distance is an island."

"That's not possible," put in Jennifer, "There were no islands any where near the spot John marked on the map."

"Perhaps John has strayed off course," I suggested.

"Not a chance," Michael answered, "I've checked our heading several times since we left. He's spot on where we should be."

The island was small and tropical in nature, roughly oval in shape, and no more than four or five miles across at its widest point. We conducted an initial journey around the island, keeping the boat at a safe distance from the rugged shorelines. We saw no evidence that a boat had run aground, and no flotsam littered the water.

"Perhaps they're on the island," Jennifer suggested.

"How did they get there?" Rob asked. "Doesn't look like there's anywhere someone could safely make it onto land—"

The words had barely left his lips when we came around a craggy bend and found ourselves greeted by a beautiful expanse of white sandy beach bordered by dense vegetation. Off to one side, a few yards in from the shoreline, lay a small rowboat, heavily scuffed, with several large cracks visible on its hull.

"Jesus, someone actually made it onto the island," Michael said in disbelief.

"Perhaps," I added doubtfully. "The boat looks pretty beat-up and weathered. It may have been there for months, or even a year. It's more likely that the folks who sent the original SOS managed to leave the area. Besides..." I added after reflecting further, "if anyone did make it onto the island, how'd they get the SOS signal to us? You'd need a radio to do that."

We remained silent for awhile, mesmerized by the sight of the solitary boat on the sandy shore, each of us wondering about the events that lead it there. It was Jennifer who spoke first;

"It's awfully quiet," she noted. "You would think such a lush jungle would be teaming with life. I don't see a single bird."

John, who had been piloting the boat until now, came out of the pilothouse to draw our attention to the hour, remarking, "It's getting late in the afternoon. I think we have to make a call on whether we take a quick look around the island on the slim chance anyone is still there—dead or alive."

"We've come this far," I said, "might as well go ashore and do a quick search."

The anchor was dropped at our current location, with John agreeing to remain with the boat while the rest of us went ashore. We inflated the pair of dinghies that Michael's dad had prudently placed in the galley prior to our journey. I took a knapsack with me that I had previously packed with a few emergency provisions, including water, a first aid kit and hunting knife. John handed me one of the walkie talkies before we departed. "Let me know what you find," he added. I nodded and gave him the thumbs up as I left to join the others.

"And Mark..." I stopped and turned to face him from the doorway. "Be on your guard," he cautioned me.

We left the dinghies next to the old rowboat before making our way slowly towards the dense foliage that bordered the beach.

"I don't see how we're going to make our way through this," commented Jennifer, "We'd need a machete to hack our way through."

"Over there," Rob said, pointing to our left, "between those two palm trees that cross over each other. There's a clearing that looks like the beginning of a pathway." He proved to be correct, and in a few minutes we were making our way along a narrow path, enveloped in an oppressive humidity and an eerie stillness, the only sounds being our footsteps and the occasional crack of a twig or branch underfoot. We continued on for a further twenty minutes before the trail came to an abrupt end at the base of a large palm tree.

"There's no one on this island," Rob said as he wiped the sweat from his brow with the bottom of his t-shirt. "Let's head on back."

"Hold on," said Michael, who was examining the tree carefully. "Someone's made a series of notches that alternate on either side of the trunk, and they appear to go all the way to the top. Any volunteers to climb up?"

"Don't bother," I said. "You can see from down here that no one's up there. I agree with Rob, this island is deserted. Let's head back to the boat. We should aim to get back to port before nightfall."

We had just made our way back onto the beach, not more than a couple of feet from the entrance of the footpath, when Jennifer tripped over something protruding from the ground. I grabbed her arm to steady her and turned to see what she had stumbled over. It looked like the toe tip of a shoe, specifically a deck shoe, with its characteristic leather lacing. We were all wearing a pair, and, quite idiotically, looked at each other to see if any us had lost a shoe. Feeling a touch of embarrassment, I chuckled and stated, "Well, that's certainly not one of ours."

I reached down and grabbed the shoe. It did not give easily. I suddenly felt my stomach turn as I pulled the shoe upward once more and exposed an ankle in the process.

"Jesus!" I burst out, stumbling back a few steps. "There's a body under there!"

"Oh my God!" Jennifer cried, taking hold of my arm with a trembling hand.

"But...but...there's no way it could have been here when we first came through," Rob stammered in disbelief.

Michael had remained silent, but I followed his horror stricken gaze out to sea, towards the direction of our boat. It had drifted further away from shore. A feeling of dread crept over me as I swung my knapsack forward and rummaged frantically through its contents until I found the walkie talkie.

"Come in, John. Over."

No response.

"Goddammit, John!" I yelled in panic, my heart racing. "Pick up the damn receiver, do you hear me?"

No reply.

I let the walkie talkie fall by my side as I reluctantly turned towards the body buried in the sand. The others watched motionless and dumbfounded as I dropped to one knee and, using my hands, started to brush away the sand from the spot where I guessed the head to be. Moments later, I revealed the face underneath, and it belonged to John.

A sense of foreboding filled the air around us as we fixed our attention on John's face, encircled solely by white sand. *This can't be happening*, I foolishly tried telling myself, unable to shake the sense of unreality I was experiencing. But the sight of John's ghastly face made it clear that the horror of the situation was undeniably real. *Only one thing to do now—get everyone back on the boat, then radio for help.*

"Michael," I began, trying to keep my voice as calm as possible, "you and Jenifer head over to the dinghies and get them to the shoreline ready for departure. Rob and I will deal with the body."

As the two of us lifted John out of the sand, I noticed something clasped in his hand. It was the small, black idol Rob had found earlier in the day. I took it and handed it to him, who, not knowing what to do with it, dropped it in his pocket. As there wasn't room for the body in the dinghy, we placed it in the underbrush next to the trail intending to come back for it later. We made our way back to the shoreline. I could tell Jennifer was holding back tears, as she whispered, gravely, "The dinghies...ripped apart..."

"Ripped apart..." I repeated slowly in disbelief.

"I'm getting off the island now!" Rob broke out suddenly. "I'm going to swim out to the boat. I recommend you all come with me."

I shook my head and said, "Not a good idea, Rob. We need to stay together, here, until the morning."

"Are you crazy? Someone's trying to kill us. We need to get off this damn island now!"

"Stop and think, Rob. It's going to be nightfall soon. Look how far off the boat has drifted. You'll be swimming in the dark, in shark infested waters. You won't stand a chance."

Rob stared out at the boat and let out a deep breath before looking back at me. "What do you suggest?" he asked, his voice a little calmer.

"We build a huge bonfire and stay by it all night. There's time still to collect enough wood in the few minutes of sunlight we have left. In the morning, we put together a few fallen logs and build a raft. It just needs to be sturdy enough to get you to *The Osprey*. From there you send an SOS and then head here to get us, even if that means beaching the damn boat. There's enough water and tinned food for a couple of days on board. We'll be rescued well before then."

"Listen to Mark," put in Michael, "It's our best chance. We have to stay together."

Rob cast his eyes towards the boat once again as he thought it over before replying. "Alright," he said somewhat reluctantly, "let's start collecting some wood."

Rob grabbed the largest log he could find and started to drag it towards the beach. "This should burn for hours. You guys collect as much material as you can to start the fire." I watched him for a few moments as he made his way in the direction of the old boat.

Dusk had fallen suddenly after a few minutes of collecting twigs and branches. I removed the flashlight from my knapsack and used it to guide us towards the silhouette of the rowboat. I called out for Rob, but there was no answer.

"For God's sake!" I cried out loud, "Tell he me he didn't try it!"

We ran and found his clothes and shoes discarded beside the rowboat.

"Rob!" I shouted once more, sweeping the flashlight's beam across the surface of the water. I could hear him swimming, and soon the light caught his figure about thirty feet out.

He turned and gave me the thumbs up as he yelled, "Be back in no time!" And then I saw him suddenly disappear, as if something had grabbed him from beneath the water. He did not resurface.

The three of us returned to the path and placed Rob's clothes next to John's body, the idol falling out of Rob's pants pocket as we did so. Michael picked it up before asking me what we should do with it. I told him to throw it in the sea. "I don't think Rob would have wanted us to," he replied, pocketing the object.

Returning to the woodpile, we worked silently, almost in a state of numbness, as we built up the fire so that the circle of firelight extended for several feet all around us. We sat with our backs resting against the weathered rowboat. I agreed to take first watch, having removed the hunting knife from my bag and strapping it onto my belt. I did this more for Jennifer's and Michael's peace of mind, as I felt it would be of no use against the malevolence we faced here.

Jennifer was right about the island being uncannily quiet. The usual chatter of nocturnal insects was missing, leaving just the occasional crackle of the flames and the gentle lapping of water against the sandy beach. It was this latter sound that caught my attention shortly after the others had gone to sleep. It seemed to me that the sound of the waves washing ashore grew louder. I reached for the flashlight beside me and shone the beam at the coastline. The water was rising rapidly, and the waves were getting bigger, crashing down with greater force.

I shook Jennifer and Michael awake. "Get up! The water's rising fast, we need to get to the path." I had just finished uttering these words as the water from a crashing wave surged forward splashing onto the fire, causing it to hiss and steam.

We ran in the general direction of the path, and soon my flashlight illuminated the intersecting palm trees that marked its entrance. "Get to the tree at the end of the path," I shouted over my shoulder. We were already running in water that was ankle-deep, and by the time we reached the end of the trail the water had risen to our knees.

We used the notches carved in the tree to climb up its trunk. Jennifer went first, and Michael insisted I follow her. "Give me the flashlight," he said, "I'll point it upwards as I follow right behind you." We were twenty feet up with the water just a few feet beneath us. There was a sudden backwash of the water below us, as when water retreats after a wave breaks on shore, only to be followed by the roar of rushing water and snapping branches. Michael pointed the flashlight in the direction of the approaching sound. A huge wave was coming our way, carrying with it *The Osprey*.

We were directly in the boat's path, it's bow hitting the tree seconds later, the sudden impact sending Jennifer and me tumbling onto the boat's deck below. I hit the metal railing on the starboard side as I landed, fracturing my ribs. The boat rocked violently from side to side as we made our way into the pilothouse on hands and knees before collapsing next to the wooden bench.

Morning, and I awoke to the sound of silence. Jennifer was still asleep. The boat was afloat but listing slightly on its port side. The sea was dead calm, and there was no sign that the island had ever existed.

I made my way onto the deck, the pain from my fall causing me to grimace with each step. Michael was at the bow, his head slumped forward and only his torso visible above the railing. As I approached, I could see that the spar extending from the front of the boat had impaled him through the chest. His arms hung loosely forward, with one hand clenched shut. I knew what it held.

I removed the idol from his grasp and regarded it with a sense of revulsion. "What kind of pagan evil are you? Are three lives not enough?" As if in answer to my question, I noticed its carved necklace featured four shells. Three were now pointing upwards towards its open mouth, the fourth pointed downwards.

"I see...still one more..."

Sickened by its sight, I pocketed the idol and made my way back to the pilothouse. Jennifer was awake, and asked me if Michael was dead. I nodded my head slightly before I made my way over to the radio and switched it on. There was only static. I retrieved the map from beneath it, knowing that John always stored it there.

"It's going to be alright, Jennifer. The antenna has been knocked over but it's still attached. I'm sure I can reconnect it. Do you know how to send a MAYDAY?

"Yes, I remember how."

"Good. Our coordinates are on the border of the map, which I left next to the radio. When I rap on the roof you go ahead and send out the MAYDAY."

"Mark—"

I didn't let her finish. "Trust me," I interrupted, "it will work." She gave me a faint smile as I left the cabin.

I climbed the ladder to the pilothouse roof and headed over to the antenna, knowing that I would find it perfectly upright and undamaged. I drew my hunting knife out from its holder and rapped on the roof three times with the base of its handle. Reluctantly, I removed the idol from my pocket and uttered, "You'll have your fourth sacrifice..." I cast the vile thing into the sea, then severed my throat with the cold, sharp blade.

"MAYDAY, MAYDAY, MAYDAY, this is *The Osprey.*" Jennifer released the transmit button and waited. A reply came moments later.

"MAYDAY received *Osprey*, please give coordinates."

Jennifer's eyes filled with tears of joy as she shouted, "Mark, come down, quick! You were right, everything is going to be alright. We're going home!"

PEARLY WHITES

Chicago, 1905

"There must be a way," George pondered as he sipped his lukewarm coffee at his workbench. He fancied himself an inventor and had set up a workshop in his basement, or as his wife liked to point out, *her* basement in *her* house. She was right, of course, he had very little in the way of property or money when he married her. But he had good looks and plenty of charm, which went a long way in getting her to notice him at ballroom dances held at the city's fashionable hotels. It was love at first sight for Dora, and after courting her for six months, he proposed. Unfortunately, her father saw right through his intentions, realizing he was just after her fortune, and so was dead set against the marriage and refused to give his consent. And then fate intervened, as it has a habit of doing under such circumstances, and Dora's father dropped dead of a heart attack. The happy couple got married a few weeks later.

At first, the marriage was an amicable one. George paid attention to her needs, and she agreed to support him financially, as he worked on his inventions. He told her about some of the great projects he was working on (like the 'Lite-O-Case', a cigarette case that automatically lights a cigarette when the case is opened) and how they would be wealthy beyond her imagination when he finally launched his products to the eager public. But soon Dora came to the sad realization that George was not a great inventor, and that he had no interest in doing anything more productive than tinkering with his childish contraptions. Father was right, he married her for her money.

"George," she said one morning at breakfast, "I'm sorry to say that I can no longer afford to fund your workshop."

"But...but...I'm so close to perfecting several of my projects," he stammered.

"You said the same last month," Dora replied matter-of-factly, "and the month before that, and the month previous to that. I must be frank with you, George, that in my opinion, there is the least likelihood that any of your inventions will come to fruition, much less make us money. No, I've quite made up my mind that I cannot fund your work any longer. From now on, if you require money in order to proceed with your inventions, you'll have to go out and earn it."

After staring at her blankly for a few moments, George nodded his head in agreement as he set his knife and fork down.

"Of course you are right, you have been patient enough with me. I will go out and make a proper living. I'll begin inquiries next week."

Dora's expression softened and a faint smile crossed her lips. "Thank you for understanding, George. It's very decent of you. If I can help in any way as you begin your search for a job, please let me know."

"Thank you, dear. Give me a day or two to think about it. Perhaps one or two of your influential friends can make a few introductions for me."

George could tell she was pleased with his response as she went back to eating her toast and jam, chatting away about their neighbour's new automobile. Little did she know that just a few moments earlier he had decided to murder her.

Some days later, Dora and George were invited to a dinner at the Williams'. Dora reminded her husband that Frank Williams' engineering business was growing and that he should inquire, discreetly of course, if there was an opportunity for him at the firm. She reasoned that an inventor like himself must know quite a lot about engineering, so the request would not appear to be unreasonable.

Dinner proved to be an excellent affair, certainly one of the better meals George had had in a while, which included clam chowder, cod with oyster sauce, roast beef and a steamed pudding with brandy sauce for dessert. *This is the life for me,* thought George as he finished sipping his wine. *I could enjoy such luxury if I could do away with Dora.*

After dinner, the two men retired to the library to enjoy a whiskey and smoke cigars. George's eye was caught by the large, leather-bound book with metal clasps on the edge of Frank's desk. He had seen similar books during his youth, and most recently at the university's rare book room. *Must be worth a pretty penny*, he reflected.

"Are you a collector of antique books?" George inquired casually.

Frank shot a surprised look at George before replying. "You mean that cursed thing sitting at the edge of my desk? I wish I had never set eyes on it."

"Why do you say that?"

"I presume you've read about Farwell's passing away recently. It's been in all the major papers."

"Yes, I have. He passed away suddenly of a heart attack at the age of fifty. But what does he have to do with the book?"

Frank walked over and handed George a glass of whiskey, before stating, "Have a seat and I'll fill you in on what I happen to know about the circumstances surrounding his death, and how that book came into my possession."

George seated himself in the leather armchair in front of the desk. Frank took a seat in the other chair, angling it so that he faced George.

"As reported by the newspapers," Frank began, "he died of a heart attack, but the authorities never questioned what triggered the heart attack. I knew Farwell quite well, a brilliant businessman but the fool dabbled in the dark arts. I think it all nonsense, of course, but I don't mind telling you, some of the stories Farwell told me made me feel mighty uneasy. Conjuring up demons and the like." Frank paused at this point to take a long sip of his whiskey.

"When I went to pay my condolences to his wife, Ruth, the day after his passing," he continued, "she told me that he died with a horrible expression of fear on his face and that the book lay on the desk next to his slumped body. There was a slight splattering of blood on the page at which it lay open, a page that depicted a cloaked figure, 'something ungodly', as she put it, 'not of this world'. Naturally, Ruth didn't want the authorities to know anything about her husband's obsession with the occult, so she shut the book and moved it to the bookshelf before their arrival. She couldn't bear to be in the same house as the book, so she implored me to take it with me when I left. The poor woman was almost in a state of hysteria when she asked me. So you see, there was nothing for me to do but agree to her request and take that vile thing with me upon my departure."

George was fascinated by the story. It never occurred to him to turn to the occult for the solution to what has been constantly on his mind these past few days—how to rid himself of Dora.

"That's quite an unsettling story. I can see now why you don't want that book in your home."

Frank nodded his head in agreement, lit his cigar, then tossed the box of matches over to George. Both men took a few puffs in silence before George spoke;

"I might be able to help you dispose of the book. I have a friend who works at the university library. He knows a great deal about old texts. He could tell me if it has any monetary value, which I suspect it does. Perhaps the university itself would be interested in purchasing it for its rare book collection. You could offer the proceeds to Farwell's wife, or to charity, if she felt uneasy about accepting the money."

"That's a fine idea you have there, George. I think I'll take you up on the offer. Heaven knows I'll sleep better at night knowing it's gone from here."

"Excellent. If it's alright with you, I'll pick it up tomorrow afternoon." After a brief pause, George leaned forward and added in a lower tone, "By the way, Dora is very impressionable and I'd rather she didn't know anything about our arrangement. Poor woman wouldn't sleep a wink if she knew such a book existed."

"I completely understand, George. I'll have the book wrapped up in plain paper and will let the maid know that she should be expecting you tomorrow." Leaning back in his chair and stretching out his legs, Frank said, "And now that that's taken care of, tell me a little about yourself, George. Dora says you're an inventor. How's the business going?"

"Well...I wouldn't yet define it as a business..."

So pleased was Dora with how well the evening went at the Williams' that she left George alone for the remainder of the week as he retreated to his workshop downstairs. *Obviously she is under the impression that Frank thought highly of me,* reasoned George, *and that* he will reach out to discuss the possibility of employment in the near future. *Little does she know that his sole remark about my inventions was, 'Well, I suppose we all need some sort of hobby to while away the time.'* Doris was likewise unaware that George was not working on his inventions but carefully studying the volume he had collected from Frank's residence earlier that week.

Before emigrating to America at the age of fifteen, George lived with his grandparents in Germany. His grandfather was an avid collector of old books, particularly those that dealt with witchcraft and the dark arts. After his grandparents went to bed, George would sneak downstairs and peruse his grandfather's collection, especially the large tomes like the one that lay open before him now—a *grimoire*, or book of black magic spells and demonic rituals.

It was slow, tedious work searching the book for the spell he hoped it would contain, made all the more difficult as the volume was penned in German circa 1720. It was a set of three illustrations that eventually caught his attention. The first depicted a body of a naked man in a shallow tub filled with what appeared to be water. A cloaked figure stood next to the tub, clutching a small urn in his skeletal hand. The second illustration depicted the figure pouring the contents of the urn into the water, which had turned red and foamy, completely engulfing the body. In the final illustration, the water was once again clear, and there was no sign of the body. George translated the caption below the illustrations as, "Eliminating all traces of a body, living or dead."

"This is too good to be true," George said excitedly, "I could rid myself of Dora and not a trace of her body would ever be found. Even if the police came to suspect me of doing away with her, the total absence of her body would make a conviction impossible."

George spent the better part of the following day translating the text. Obtaining the elements required for the potion would not be difficult, with the exception of one item. The final element made George recoil in horror. He broke out in a cold sweat, felt light-headed, nauseous, and gasped for air. George was hemophobic—he had an intense, irrational fear of blood, and the final ingredient of the spell required a bone from a living or recently deceased person. As the text was written in the early eighteenth century, it recommended bribing body snatchers for a finger or toe from one of their excavated cadavers before they sold it to medical schools for dissection, or, failing that, the corpse of an executed criminal was another possible source, as the executioner could easily be bribed to turn a blind eye as a finger was severed from the body.

George collected himself for a few minutes before gathering the courage to read the final two lines of the spell, which roughly translated to, *Should no corpse be available, the individual administering the potion may use one of their own body parts containing a bone, such as the severed tip of a finger from their hand.* George gasped before slumping forward in a faint, his head hitting the hard surface of the workbench.

He came to a few minutes later, the ringing of the dinner bell stirring him awake. The side of his temple ached, and he could tell it was swollen as he ran his hand gently across it. The pain only added to his feeling of discontent. Here before him sat the solution to his problem, yet his irrational fear of blood prevented him from implementing it. His vision of a rich, carefree future was not to be.

"Why, George," said Dora as George seated himself at the dinner table, "whatever happened to your head? You have a goose egg on your left side."

"It's nothing, dear," he assured her. "Hit my head on the workbench as I reached down to retrieve something I knocked over onto the floor. The swelling will be gone by the morning."

"I do hope so, dear." Dora cleared her throat gently before asking, casually, "Have you heard from Frank Williams?"

"I'm doing a bit of research for him at the university. We are to meet again next week."

"Oh, that is good news. I think you stand a very good chance of joining his firm," she added proudly.

He knew otherwise, but responded, "Thank you for the encouraging words, my dear. Let us hope so."

She smiled, then changed topics by asking, "I trust you haven't forgotten what next Thursday is?"

"Of course not, it's your thirtieth birthday. Is there a special gift you had in mind?"

"Why yes, there is. I thought a pearl necklace would make a lovely gift. What do you think?" she asked, smiling.

George stared at her luminous smile in awe for a moment. The phrase 'pearly whites' popped into his mind, followed by the thought, *Of course! That's the solution!* He could barely contain his enthusiasm as he responded;

"What a wonderful idea! Pearls represent wisdom, and you are a very wise woman, my dear. Yes, pearls it is!"

"Why thank you, George. You really have been a wonderful husband as of late."

"My pleasure, Dora. Now, where would you like to dine on your Birthday?"

The following morning, George complained of a toothache, and made an appointment to see his dentist that afternoon. The dentist found nothing wrong with his tooth, but George insisted that it be pulled, as the pain was unbearable. Reluctantly, the dentist did as his patient asked. George took the tooth with him when he left, having requested that it be rinsed clean of any blood beforehand. He also secreted one of the small glass bottles of chloroform in his jacket pocket as he made his way out of the office.

Back at his workstation, he carefully unwrapped his tooth and, despite the soreness from the extraction, smiled gleefully. "What a clever man you are, George," he congratulated himself. "We have thirty-two little skeletal protrusions in our mouth, and I can easily sacrifice one for a life of leisure. No need to sever a finger!" He spent the next hour preparing the formulation. Tomorrow he would dissolve Dora out of existence.

George kissed Dora on the cheek as he departed for the library. When he heard the door shut behind him he turned and headed to the rear of the house, silently entering his workshop through the basement entrance. He crept up the stairs to the second floor and stopped outside the bathroom door. Wednesday was Dora's bathing day, and he could hear her humming as she started to run the water. Removing the chloroform bottle from his jacket pocket, he applied some to his handkerchief before opening the door a crack. Dora was wearing her morning gown and her back was to the door. George rushed in, pressing the handkerchief over her mouth and nose. He had grossly underestimated her strength as Dora struggled violently to free herself. For a moment he believed she would succeed but the vapours soon had their effect, and her body slumped to the floor. He turned off the faucet before sitting on the edge of the tub to catch his breath. "That was damn close," he murmured to himself, reaching for the nearby towel to wipe the sweat from his brow.

He disrobed her and placed her body in the bathtub which was half filled. Removing the vial from his breast pocket, he uncorked it and held it up towards Dora as a toast, "Farewell, my dear, and thanks for all your wealth."

George tipped the contents of the tube into the bath, the water foaming violently as it turned a deep crimson. He staggered out of the room as he slammed the bathroom door behind him. He was perspiring and gasping for air. *Good God,* he thought, *was that blood that filled the tub? It couldn't be; it happened too suddenly, it must have been a chemical reaction,* he assured himself. He changed into different clothes, disposed of the chloroform handkerchief, and headed to the library to visit his friend. *Best to invite Henry out to lunch,* he reasoned on the way over, *strengthens my alibi if I'm seen in public. In fact, I should head over to the club immediately after to play cards and billiards, and not return home until nine or ten.*

George returned at half-past nine that evening, calling out Dora's name as he stepped through the doorway, tentatively at first, then once again louder. There was no response. He made his way to the bathroom, his heart beating quicker as he pushed the door open and reached for the light switch.

Dora's robe still lay on the ground. He walked over to the tub. It was half-filled with clear water and there was not a trace of Dora. He stared at the tub in disbelief as the realization that he was a wealthy man finally dawned on him. He laughed and raised his arms in triumph before a blow to the base of his neck rendered him unconscious.

"My aching head," George said under his breath as he struggled to open his eyes. He slowly came to the realization that he was lying in a bathtub, the warm water comforting his sore body. It took him a few more moments to notice someone else was in the room, as he tried to focus on the figure opposite him.

"Ah, you're finally coming round," said Dora, who was sitting on the rim of the bathtub next to the faucets. "You must have one doozy of a headache after I slugged you with a rolling pin. You didn't stay unconscious for long though, so I had to give you the same chloroform treatment you gave me. I needed some time to bind your hands and feet before I lugged your body into the tub."

"Dora?" George asked stupidly.

"In the flesh," she replied with a smile. "You see George, I caught sight of your reflection in the mirror as you attacked me. So when I came to and found myself in a bathtub, unharmed, I knew whatever scheme you had planned to do away with me had failed. Naturally the police would never believe me if I went to them with such a tale. Instead, I took the small pistol I keep hidden in my drawer and went looking for you. You were out, of course, but I came across your scribblings on your workbench, along with the bottle of chloroform. After reading your notes, I decided to give you a taste of your own medicine. So here you are, in the bathtub with your hands and feet bound."

The fog in his brain had begun to clear, and George realized his only hope of getting out of this mess was to console her using his charm. "Dora, my dear, it's not at all what you think. Let me explain—"

"I'm not through yet, George," interrupted Dora. "I think you should know you made an error in the preparation of your formula."

George scoffed at the very idea.

"But you did," went on Dora. "I remember chatting away with my dentist on one particular visit and, I can't remember how we got on the topic, he told me that teeth are not part of our skeletal system. In fact, they are not considered bones at all. So, I made up a small batch of the formula as it was originally intended."

Dora held up a vial she had been holding in her hands.

For a moment, a sense of foreboding overtook George as he counted the fingers on each of her hands while she uncorked the vial. *They're all there! Foolish woman, probably used a chicken bone.* A wry smile crept across his face.

"Don't look so smug, George," Dora said, as if discerning his thoughts, "I used one of *your* fingers."

The blood drained from his face as he lifted his bound hands clear of the water and saw that the tip of his right pinky had been severed.

Dora flashed him a radiant smile before adding, "Let's see what happens, shall we?"

She poured the contents of the vial into the bathtub. As before, the water foamed violently and turned a deep crimson hue, this time from the blood of George's dissolving body.

CHARLES LINKWOOD

London, 1918

S hell Shock. That's what the doctors call it when you witness hell on earth...

My battalion arrived at the Western Front in October of 1917. Orders from the British High Command directed us to breach the German defenses and take possession of the crucial Belgian ports under their occupation. But to reach the enemy position, we had to cross No Man's Land, a God-forsaken stretch of land, fifty yards wide, littered with decomposing bodies and severed limbs. Five days of relentless rain had turned the area into a quagmire, and the water within the huge shell-holes that spotted the landscape became reddened with the blood of fallen soldiers.

Our attack was launched close to dawn. A mist had rolled in from the coast and we were grateful for the cover it provided. It was an effort to wade through the thick mud, and I found myself falling behind the group of men I was with. I had not progressed more than twenty yards before I saw the German flare-lights illuminate the sky. I knew then that a curtain of death was about to fall upon us.

The enemy let loose a massive artillery barrage, and within seconds the air around us was full of shrapnel from the exploding shells. Men collapsed all around me, crying out in pain as limbs were torn from their bodies. A shell detonated a few yards to my left, showering me with a heavy blanket of mud. I wiped the sludge away from my eyes and looked around in a daze, my ears ringing loudly.

I was alone, not a man left standing—fed to the enemy as mere cannon fodder. I managed to pull my legs free from the deep mud, and, with my mind clearing, continued my slow march towards the enemy. My hearing returned, and I could make out the sound of machine-gun fire, the bullets occasionally whistling by my head. To my right, I suddenly became aware of a figure moving alongside of me, a few feet away. I had a queer notion that I was dead, watching myself march forward, as a living corpse.

"Harry?" a familiar voice called out.

I stopped and peered hard at the figure. A gust of wind lifted the mist for a moment and I cried out, astonished;

"Charles! Good Lord, is it really you?"

"I daresay so, my good man," he replied almost cheerfully, "Bloody hell, at least a couple of us are still standing! Stay where you are, I'll make my way over to you." He took a single step forward before a shell exploded a short distance away, causing him to collapse backwards, his lower legs severed at the knees.

"Charles!" I shouted as I staggered towards him, the feeling that some unseen force was holding me back as the mud engulfed each of my steps. I reached his body moments later, falling to my knees beside him, exhausted. There was blood trickling from his mouth, and an ugly piece of shrapnel protruded from the side of his neck.

"For...God's sake...man," he stammered, "Finish it...please..." He held out his trembling hand which I took in my own, softly laying it on his chest before letting it go as I stood up.

He kept his deep blue eyes upon me as I pulled my revolver from its holster and aimed it at his head. I uttered a plea for divine mercy, then with an unsteady hand pulled the trigger, the bullet piercing his forehead. The last thing I recall is a look of terror overtaking his face as his eyes turned bright and fierce before closing for the last time. I raised the revolver to my temple as everything around me started to spin, and then darkness overtook me.

I was invalided to a hospital on the coast of France, suffering from extreme 'battle fatigue.' The doctors discharged me after six weeks, three of which I had spent suffering from brain fever. Deemed unfit for battle, I was shipped back to London in December, arriving home in time for Christmas. I inquired about Charles Linkwood at the War Office, but they had no record of his death, and so had marked him as 'missing in action.'

I spent a month with my sister at her Pimlico lodgings before finding furnished lodgings of my own in the St. James's district. I had by this time secured a position with the Directorate of Military Training at the War Office. My days settled down into a comfortable routine, which included an occasional gathering with a few friends at a military club. But nighttime was a different matter entirely. Many a restless night have I spent reliving the horrors I witnessed on the battlefield, and my dreams were haunted with the vision of Charles Linkwood, how my bullet extinguished his fiery blue eyes. I live with a deep guilt knowing his body was not found, that I was recovering in a hospital while hordes of rats fatten themselves on his rotting remains. *Forgive me,*

Charles. Had I been a better man, I would have had the fortitude to carry your body back to our trenches instead of attempting to end my own life. I will never forgive myself for such an act of cowardice...

The bleak, gray winter months finally yielded to the vibrant days of spring. On an especially lazy afternoon, I settled back comfortably in one of the club's lounge chairs by the open window. I watched uninterested as pedestrians and carriages made their way along the avenue, occasionally interrupted by the sight of a motor vehicle. A well dressed man in a double breasted striped suit and Derby hat suddenly darted across the street, narrowly avoiding being hit by two carriages traveling in opposite directions.

Reckless fool, I mused, *almost did away with his life.*

I kept my eye on the man as he continued his walk across the street from me. He stopped to tip his hat as he greeted a passing gentleman, and at that moment I caught a glimpse of his eyes. I started back all at once as a sense of unreality overtook me. "Good God," I uttered in shock, "it's not possible!"

The next minute I was outside the club, hurrying down the street, all the while searching for the man in the Derby hat. The sidewalks were crowded, and I had to apologize on more than one occasion as I tried to navigate around those walking by. I was about to cross the road when a strong hand gripped my arm and pulled me back just as a carriage sped past. I turned to thank the man and found myself staring into the piercing blue eyes of Charles Linkwood.

"Henry!" he exclaimed with delight, "I was hoping I'd bump into you—" He broke off as his expression turned into one of concern. "My dear man, you look extremely pale. Are you not well?"

For a moment, I could find no words, so I simply answered, "Fine."

"Well, you certainly don't look it. Come, my club is not more than a five minute walk from here. Some brandy will do you good. Then we'll enjoy a couple of cigars as we catch up on everything that's happened since we got back."

We sat in silence as I took several long puffs of my cigar, Charles watching me with interest.

"Well," he said eventually, "the brandy has given you your colour back, but you still appear out of sorts. What has disturbed you so?"

"What..happened to you," I began tentatively, "at the Western Front."

"Bad show, that. As you well know, most of the men in our squadron were slaughtered within minutes of leaving our trenches. I was relieved to hear you survived, although I understand you had a rough go of it with brain fever. As for myself, I made it to the enemy line by some miracle. Didn't do me much good, as no one else made it across. Can't very well capture a well-defended seaport single-handedly. Fortunately, a group of resistance fighters became aware of my presence and eventually got me back across the line. Took a nasty bullet in my left shoulder in the process, shattered the bone. Add to that a severe bout of trench fever and my career as a soldier was over. So here I am." He took a puff of his cigar before continuing, "But, I feel much better now, and just between you and me, I pretty much have full use of my arm again."

He gave a chuckle as he rotated his shoulder a couple of times before gesturing with his cigar in my direction. "And what about you, my dear friend?" he asked, "What happened to you on the battlefield?"

I avoided his question, but instead asked, "Charles, how long have we known each other?"

"Since we were young children."

"During all those years, did you ever have reason to think of me as...mentally unbalanced?"

"Certainly not! Quite the opposite, you were always the sensible one, while I was always causing mischief." Charles looked at me pensively while he tapped the ash from his cigar. He leaned in close and, lowering his tone, asked, "Look here, Henry, what are you getting at?"

"The War Office told me you were missing in action."

"Bloody fools. They're always making a blunder of things. Wouldn't surprise me in the least if they now have me listed as a 'prisoner of war.' But I ask you again, Henry, what's this all about?"

"I saw you die on the battlefield, Charles. You were hit by shrapnel and were good as dead when I got to you. I...I finished the job with my own revolver."

Charles leaned back in his chair for a moment's reflection before stating in a calm, sympathetic voice, "Shell shock, my dear fellow. We've all returned burdened by our own demons following our experience at the front. But as you can see for yourself, I'm alive and well. Now that you know this, I hope it will rid you of those dreadful visions."

"I hope so too, Charles. My evenings have become unbearable."

Charles eyes lit up as a smile gradually appeared on his face. "I have a wonderful idea!" he exclaimed, leaning forward. "Madam Jullien is hosting an evening soiree this weekend, and I've been invited. Come with me as my guest. It will do you a world of good to socialize among the well-to-do crowd. I'm also told that there will be several eligible ladies attending. What do you say?"

"I can certainly do with an evening away from my flat. Thank you, Charles, I would be delighted to join you."

"Splendid! Meet me here at the club Saturday at half-past eight and we'll take a cab together to the event."

We were announced by the manservant and Madam Jullien left the small party of women she was conversing with to greet us. She was a stout, plain-looking woman with rich, dark hair upswept under a lace headdress. Unlike her appearance, the necklace that adorned her low neckline was anything but ordinary. Not one, but three strands of large pearls beautifully matched in size and lustrous, creamy-white colour.

She greeted us cordially, remarking how pleased she was that such brave soldiers as ourselves were among her guests. After a minute or two of polite conversation, she excused herself and made her way to greet a distinguished looking couple that had just arrived, exclaiming, "Sir Arthur and Lady Helen, how good of you to attend my little party..."

As she left us, I commented, "Those were stunning pearls. There must be very few necklaces like that in London, if not in all of Britain. Did you take note of the necklace clasp as she walked away—it had a magnificent emerald surrounded by diamonds."

"An exquisite piece. Worth a small fortune, no doubt. Mind you, her husband is an American oil baron, I'm sure he can well afford to purchase such luxury on occasion."

"I daresay he could. Must be wonderful to have such wealth."

"I agree. But enough talk of pearls, we are here to enjoy ourselves. Let me tell you the plan I've mapped out for us this evening. We drink, we find some lovely ladies to dance with, and then we drink some more. Repeat *ad infinitum.* How does that sound to you?"

"Brilliant. Better than any strategy the War Office could conceive. Let us begin with a glass of Champagne. I see a servant heading our way carrying a tray of glasses."

The evening went, more or less, according to plan. We were both tipsy by the time we left, and my feet were sore from all the dancing. Nevertheless, Charles was adamant that I should join him at his club for a nightcap, of which we had several. When I got to my flat, it was approaching half-past three in the morning, I collapsed onto my bed still half-dressed and immediately went to sleep. It was the first night that I did not dream of Charles Linkwood.

The next day, late in the afternoon, I came across Charles having tea at an outdoor cafe.

"Henry, wonderful to see you up and about so early given our late hour yesterday. Join me for a cup of tea, or coffee, if you prefer."

"Thank you, Charles, I think I will."

As I seated myself across from him, he inquired, "So, do I still haunt your dreams?"

"I am happy to report that you do not. I slept as soundly as a baby."

"Wonderful news! And speaking of news, have you seen the front page of The Standard?" He handed me the newspaper that was sitting folded next to his cup. I scanned the front page, which was dominated by news of the war save for the following headline near the bottom; 'Massacre at Thompson Manor.'

"Good Lord!," I exclaimed, after perusing the article, "Madam Jullien and her husband murdered while sleeping in their beds, and it happened in the early hours of the morning following the party."

"Butchered is more like it. I overheard a couple of reporters discussing the case at the table behind me. They said the couple was beheaded, their heads literally hacked off using a cleaver taken from their very own kitchen."

"How ghastly! The article states that the police believe robbery to be the motive. Madam Jullien's pearls were missing."

"That is curious," mused Charles. "There was no need to kill the couple if all the intruder wanted was her jewels. I'm sure the police have considered that point as they search for the culprit. I guess all the guests at the party will be questioned at some point, including us."

"Yes," I said uneasily, "I presume they will."

"Tell you what," said Charles abruptly, steering the conversation away from the murder, "let's have a game of bridge tonight at my place. I'll invite a couple of fellows from the club to join us. What do you say?"

"Yes, a game of bridge would suit me just fine. What time should I be there?"

"Best if you arrived before the others, say eight o'clock. You can help me rearrange some of the furniture so that we can position the card table closer to the centre of the room."

I arrived at the scheduled hour, and we wasted no time rearranging the furniture. I was to move the divan over a few feet to the far wall while Charles repositioned a pair of damask armchairs closer to the fireplace. The divan resisted my initial push, so I circled around and gave it a good pull from the other end. The sudden jerk caused the pillow facing me to tumble onto the floor, exposing the concealed object behind it.

"Sorry, old friend," came Charles' voice from across the room, "Very careless of me to have left it there. Didn't want you involved in this ugly business." He made his way to the divan and picked up the pearl necklace of Madam Jullien, tossing it into the drawer of a nearby side table before reaching for the bottle of brandy that was sitting on top.

"Have a seat in one of the chairs by the fireplace while I pour us both a stiff brandy. I'm sure you'll want an explanation as to why I have the dead woman's necklace."

I did as he said. I felt no fear, but before I sat down some vague premonition made me move my chair further back, so that there was at least five feet distance between the two chairs. Charles came over and handed me my brandy and then took a seat across from me.

"I see you put some extra distance between us. I don't blame you, I would probably do the same. Now, let's see, where to begin..." he reflected, before taking a sip of his drink.

"Did you kill them?" I asked suddenly.

"Yes, I killed the Thompsons," he answered simply.

"How...how could you?"

"It is my calling, Harry. I have no choice in the matter."

"You mean you suffer from shell shock, that you are not in control of your actions?"

"In a way, yes. But not in the manner you think." He paused to place his empty glass onto the floor, then leaned back in his chair before continuing. "Where to begin..." he remarked once more with a slight chuckle. "A rhetorical question, as there's only one place to begin, the place where it all started—at the Western Front. You see, Harry, what you witnessed that fateful morning really did occur, my life ended on that cursed piece of land, aided by your bullet." He sat pensively as if recalling the moment, then gathered himself and continued;

"Think of all the blood that has been spilled on that strip of land, not just by this war, but throughout history, from Roman conquests to peasant revolts. The land itself is saturated with the blood from man's dark and violent history. This has given birth to an almost tangible evil, one that has lurked in the region for a very long time. All that was required was one more violent death—my own—for it to manifest itself. It is now the domain of the devil himself, evil resides there and on that morning it took me as its first disciple. *I am evil* in the flesh, Harry, and I will spill the blood of mankind for many years to come, and enjoy doing so. At times it will be through random acts of violence, as was the case with the Thompsons, on other occasions I may find the opportunity to slaughter hundreds of people. So you see, Harry, you were correct in saying I have no choice in the matter. But it's not shell shock I suffer from, it's something far, far more monstrous."

As he spoke, I was aware of his eyes turning bright and fierce. My mind went back to the battlefield, how the same intensity shone from his eyes *after* my bullet ended his life. I became aware of his hands tightly griping the arms of the chair, his entire body tense, poised to spring forward. At that moment I understood why my instincts had led me to move my chair further away.

He sprang like a savage beast as I reached for the fireplace poker and swung it full force into his skull. He collapsed to the floor, blood rapidly escaping from his wound, collecting in a large pool around his head. I staggered to the door and left the flat, making my way home by the back alleyways. When I arrived, I washed the blood droplets from my hands and face, then fell into bed, utterly exhausted. By morning, I had made up my mind to remain in London and face the consequences of my actions. I would wait for the law to come and take me away.

But no one came that day or the day after. I perused the newspapers but found no mention of Charles' 'murder'. Then, on the third day, there was a knock at my door. I opened it to find two constables waiting outside.

"Mr. Harry Miller?" inquired the taller of the two.

"Yes, that's me. Please step inside constables."

"Thank you, Mr. Miller. This will only take a few minutes. We're investigating the Thompson murders and will need a statement as to your whereabouts after midnight following the party you attended on the evening of the twenty-fifth."

"Of course." I then proceeded to recount my actions for that evening, how I was at Charles' club until close to three in the morning, and how we shared a cab getting home, I being dropped off first.

"Thank you, Mr. Miller. Your story aligns with that of Charles Linkwood. I don't think we need bother you any further."

"You...you spoke to Charles?" I asked, trying to contain my astonishment.

"Why yes, just the other day."

"I see. I hadn't heard from him for a few days, I thought...he might have been out of town."

"He may have been, but he's back now."

"Thank you for letting me know, officer. Forgive me for keeping you longer than necessary with my questions. Have a good day, gentlemen."

"And you as well, Mr. Miller."

A week later, I departed from London and headed to the outskirts of Norwich, not having once encountered Charles prior to my departure. At Norwich, I took residence in a small, but comfortable cottage, and found employment as a clerk with the local parish council. Once again I settled down to a simple life, keeping mainly to myself, passing my leisure time fishing and occasionally venturing to Stonebarrow Hill to hunt for fossils.

The nights, as before, were not kind to me. Despite my best efforts to leave the past behind, I found myself lying awake questioning my sanity. How could I have possibly taken

Charles life, not once, but twice? Do I suffer from shell shock, or perhaps some form of profound psychosis? Only one thing felt certain to me: that Charles Linkwood, as impossible as it seemed, was still 'alive'.

With the cooler weather approaching, I decided to venture into the city centre the next morning with the purpose of purchasing some supplies at the general store, stopping first to have lunch at one of the tea rooms on account of the late hour. It was there that I perused a newspaper left behind by a previous patron.

It was with increasing dread that I read an article about a military unit that was heading to India to suppress a growing rebellion by the local tribes in the Manipur region. Certain phrases leaped from the page; "We will crush the rebellion with maximum force...The enemy should be prepared for much bloodshed...It will prove to be a short but brutal endeavor..." The accompanying photograph was of a Sergeant in full uniform, standing proud as he posed for the camera. The brim of his cap cast a shadow over his eyes, but it could not mask their fierce and penetrating nature, the same eyes that stared at me a few weeks ago—those of Charles Linkwood.

God have mercy on the poor souls of the Manipur people, I murmured, *it will be a slaughter.* I folded the newspaper and left it on the table.

Once home, I unlocked the bottom drawer of the desk and pulled out my service revolver. At one time, I could not forgive myself for what I saw as an act of cowardice; abandoning Charles' body on the battlefield. But I see now I am guilty of far worse. I have set an abomination loose on mankind, the beginning of what may become an ever growing army of evil. True, it may be that all I've experienced is the result of shell shock, but either way, there is only one path forward.

"I've tried killing you twice, Charles, may the third time be a charm for me." I placed the barrel of the revolver to my temple with a steady hand and declared, "By committing this moral sin, I guarantee my damnation. I will destroy you when I see you in hell, Charles."

This time, I did not fail to pull the trigger.

AN IMPRINT OF EVIL

London, UK, 1888

On a clear spring day, I received a letter offering me a post as a junior physicist at University College London. The remuneration was poor, but as I had failed to find any other employment since January of that year, I readily accepted the position, one that entailed conducting my own research as well as lecturing and tutoring undergraduates, a necessary evil associated with any junior appointment.

I began my duties in August, and within a brief period, I had set up a modest work area inside the laboratory of Professor Balfour, the senior faculty member whom I was assisting. The days were long, but I did not mind the hours, as I was young and my research gave me a great sense of satisfaction, knowing that I was helping to advance the field of electro-magnetism. Then, early one morning, at the start of second term, Professor Balfour called me into his office.

"Have a seat, Robert, and help yourself to as many biscuits as you wish. My wife insisted I take the entire lot with me this morning as she has decided to adopt a healthier food regime and does not want to be tempted by their presence at home."

I thanked him and took three, not having had breakfast that morning.

"Now that you've had the time to make the acquaintance of several of the other physicists in the department, what is your opinion of Professor William Taylor?"

"He strikes me as a very intelligent and amiable man. He's dropped by the lab on occasion while I was working late and was kind enough to express interest in my research."

"Yes, he's told me as much. Professor Taylor has recently taken an interest in what some call 'psychical research', applying scientific methods to the study of—how should I put it—the *paranormal*." He uttered this last word with a subtle hint of disapproval.

"He asked if I would be interested in helping him with his work," the professor continued, "but I declined." He paused a moment to let this last word sink in, then leaned forward from behind his desk, adding in a lowered tone, "I'll be straight with you, Robert, I have no time for such tomfoolery myself. However, since you are new here and have no scientific reputation to protect, you may find the experience a worthwhile one, as you would be compensated financially for your time. Mind you, you are expected to work on this project only outside of your regular research and teaching hours."

And that is how I came to work for Professor William Taylor and to forever regret having done so.

My first official meeting with Professor Taylor occurred one week later at eight-thirty in the evening. I arrived at the appointed time only to discover that two other individuals were already seated in his office. One was a tall, broad-shouldered young man with round spectacles that complemented his lean, square-jawed face. The professor introduced him as his assistant, Allen Foster. The other was the most beautiful woman I had ever set eyes on. She had a round face with sensuous, heart-shaped lips and large, haunting eyes. Soft brown curls flowed down the base of her neck from under her hat. It was the professor's voice that broke in on my thoughts as I stood there, captivated by her beauty.

"Robert Evans, I would like to introduce you to Miss Dorothy Hill."

I took her outstretched hand and bowed slightly. "A pleasure to meet you, Miss Hill."

"Likewise, Mr. Evans," she replied warmly.

"Miss Hill is a spiritual medium, a remarkable one, as I hope you will soon discover. Take a seat next to me, Robert, and I'll let Miss Hill tell us about her recent experiences in her own words."

"Thank you, professor. Let me begin by assuring you gentlemen that I do not, and have no intention of, profiting from my special abilities. I am here to help those poor souls who seek final closure for the tragic deaths they experienced on this earth, deaths that only their perpetrators know about."

"Murder victims," I uttered in surprise.

"That is correct, Mr. Evans. I became aware of my gift, for that is what I believe it to be, two years ago, at the age of nineteen. My cousin and I were walking along the edge of the large pond that is situated next to the gardens of Jackson Manor. We had been walking for a quarter hour when I heard a sorrowful voice call out for help. I looked around but could see no one. My cousin looked at me strangely and asked what was wrong. 'Did you not hear the call for help?' I asked anxiously. She did not, but as I stood there, I had a vision of a woman's body submerged in the pond. I walked to the very edge of the water and would have fallen in had my cousin not grabbed my arm at the last moment. 'What are you doing?' she asked in alarm. I did not reply to her question, but asked her to walk me home.

"The next day, I foolishly went to the police with my story, who tried to appease me by telling me I had experienced a 'vivid dream', one which I 'mistook' for reality. I knew otherwise, and at that moment saw it as my duty to have that poor woman's body recovered. I went to my uncle, a lawyer at Harris-Lee, and recounted my experience. He was very interested in my account. 'You say this occurred by the Jackson Manor?' he asked. When I confirmed this, he inquired if I could describe the drowned woman. I gave a slight shudder before replying that she had blond hair, was about my height, was wearing a red or burgundy dress, had a crucifix around her neck, and a terrible gash on her forehead just above her right eye.

His manner became very serious as I recounted my experience, and when I was through, he instructed me to return home and get a good night's rest, as he would have a carriage at my door for eight the next morning that would take me to the pond, where he would be waiting."

"And did he send the carriage?" I asked, captivated by her narrative.

"Why, of course. He had hired two men to drag the bottom of the pond with grappling hooks in the vicinity where I experienced my vision. They found the body a half-hour later. A large wound was above her right eye, and a crucifix was plainly visible around her neck."

"How dreadful," I murmured under my breath. "And has the woman been identified?"

"It was Lord Jackson's wife, Lady Audrey, who, incidentally, was purported to be traveling on the continent, according to her husband. That is why my uncle took such interest in my story, as my description of the woman matched that of Lady Audrey. Moreover, for days, gossip had been circulating among the servants that no one saw her depart for the journey, nor assisted in preparing her steamer trunk. Two weeks after the discovery of the body, her husband was charged with murder, found guilty, and executed."

"Truly remarkable," Allen said after a moment's pause. "And since then, have you found other victims?"

"Yes, an Inspector Berryman has, unlike his fellow officers, taken a keen interest in my ability. This past year, he has called upon me to visit other suspected crime scenes, where I was spoken to by the spirit of a child who was beaten to death by his parents and buried in their cellar, and by that of a domestic helper who was robbed and murdered for a few shillings, her body dumped into a deep well."

The professor thanked Dorothy for recounting her experiences, then addressed Allen and me, asking, "Do either of you gentlemen question the authenticity of her account?"

We both shook our heads in the negative.

"Then let me explain what I have in mind," he continued, as he rose from his chair and began to pace the room. "I would like to investigate, by scientific means whenever possible, Miss Hill's unique gift. I know science scoffs at the very mention of the paranormal, but I, like numerous others, believe it to exist. I plan, with your help, to record and gather enough tangible evidence to present to the scientific community in the hope that others will initiate their own research as well. We owe it to humanity to rationally explain what are currently inexplicable events."

"But professor," I began after briefly considering his words, "as the murder location remains unknown to all except the murderer, I don't see how we can investigate such an event. It may take months, if ever, before Miss Hill happens by chance alone to come upon such a spot. And I don't see Inspector Berryman allowing us to trample about on a possible crime scene if he should request Miss Hill's services."

The professor nodded in agreement. "Everything you say is correct, Robert, that is why I have a very specific location in mind—The Burwick House."

A profound silence fell upon the room.

"A haunting..." I said uneasily, as I recalled the accounts I read in the local newspapers concerning the house.

The professor returned to his seat and looked at us with a faint smile, commenting, "Your silence tells me that you are all familiar with the history of the place."

"I recall the newspapers covered the story in some detail," I replied. "I believe it was August of last year that the Burwick family emigrated from New York on the ill-fated Cunard steamer *Etruria*, ill-fated because three murders were committed on the journey. The victims were all women, one of whom was Mrs. Burwick's sister. They had all been strangled, their necks permanently stained black by the hands of the killer, whose identity, to this day, remains unknown."

"Your memory serves you well, Robert," the professor remarked, taking up the story from there. "Upon their arrival, the family took lodgings in one of the terraced houses in a poor suburban neighbourhood. Shortly thereafter, a woman was found dead in a nearby alleyway, strangled, the killer's black hand marks visible on her neck.

"Naturally, suspicion fell on Mr. Burwick, but the evidence showed that his large hands did not match the marks on the woman's throat, and his wife swore under oath that he had been home the evening of the murder. The following week, Mr. Burwick told the landlord that he would be vacating the premises. His wife had already left for Hastings to stay with friends they had met on their voyage here. His friend had secured employment for him at the local mill, and he was expected to report for work the next morning. From that day forward, Burwick House, as it came to be known, was haunted."

"Haunted how, professor?" asked Dorothy.

"The neighbours heard rapid knocking on their walls, doors slamming shut, and most alarming, house tremors powerful enough to cause the china to rattle. Anyone who was foolish enough to rent the place left after only a few days, claiming they could sense an evil presence, one that sought to slowly 'choke' the life out of them."

Dorothy gave the professor a puzzled look as she said, "Forgive me, professor, but I don't see how I can be of help to you at the Burwick House. There is no murder victim that can try to communicate with me."

"On that point I disagree with you, Miss Hill," came the professors' unexpected response. "A good friend of mine is a journalist who covered the story in some detail. He told me in confidence that the coroner believed that the marks on the throats of the murdered victims *were made by a woman*. The police refused to believe that a woman could carry out such a violent crime, and his opinion was never entered at the inquest."

"A woman," I repeated in disbelief. "Professor, you're not suggesting that it was..." I found myself unable to finish the sentence.

"That's precisely what I am suggesting, Robert. That Mrs. Burwick was responsible for the killings, including that of her own sister. I'm sure Mr. Burwick must have had his suspicions during their voyage. Then, when another murder took place near their residence so soon after their arrival, he could only conclude that his wife was the culprit. He took the law into his own hands and murdered her, concealing her body somewhere in the house. I believe it is her spirit that is haunting Burwick House, and that this can be verified with the help of Miss Hill's special gift."

All eyes turned toward Dorothy as she sat there silently, her dark eyes focused on the professor, his impassive expression not changing as she considered his request. "You can depend on me, professor," she said in a determined tone. "I will be there when you need me."

The professor nodded his appreciation. "Thank you, Miss Hill. You are too caring a soul not to have agreed." Turning his attention to myself and Allen, he said, "I will arrange to have access to Burwick House for Thursday evening. That gives us three days to prepare."

There was only the dim light of the moon's rays to guide our carriage down the deserted street, where every house we passed looked identical to its neighbours, each standing a short distance from the road. The Burwick House was located near the end of a long row of two-storey houses. It was a narrow house; its windows were without blinds, and cracks were visible in the brickwork. A vine crept up one corner of the house, having made its way to the upper-level window. A street water pump stood directly in front, a reminder that running water was a luxury in such impoverished neighbourhoods.

The coachman waited impatiently as Allen and I unloaded the wooden crate housing our equipment. When we were through, he tipped his hat at us and said in his gruff voice, "No business of mine, but I venture you lot are either very brave or very foolish. I guess you'll find out soon enough." With a flick of the reins, the horses trotted forward and the carriage soon disappeared down the street.

"I guess we will," replied the professor under his breath, looking up at the house.

"Why don't I go in first, professor?" I inquired, interrupting his thoughts. "I can light a few candles, then the rest of you can follow. It's a small dwelling, won't take more than a few minutes."

"Thank you for offering, Robert. Confine yourself to the first floor. The estate agent told me there are only two rooms on each floor. The front entrance opens to a parlor room, beyond which is a small dining area with kitchen."

The professor handed over the key, while Allen retrieved a handful of candles from the crate. Dorothy gave me a smile, but I thought I detected a glimmer of fear in her dark eyes as I turned and made my way to the front door.

A cool but stagnant air greeted me as I entered the house. I stood motionless for a few moments, letting my eyes adjust to the darkness before I lit the first candle. The parlor was bare, except for a small, musty-looking sofa positioned against one wall. I let a few drops of candle wax drip to the floor before pressing the base of the candle into the wax so that it would hold it in place. I repeated this with the other candles I held, placing two more in the parlor and one in each of the dining area and kitchen, then I returned to the entrance and motioned for the others to enter.

Once inside, we stood near the doorway as Dorothy slowly made her way around the first floor. "I sense a presence," she said slowly as she came back towards us. "One that has left an imprint of evil." She gave a slight shudder as she turned towards the narrow staircase. "It's on the second floor. I can hear it beckoning me."

The professor went and stood next to her, placing a hand gently upon her shoulder as he whispered reassuringly, "You don't have to go through with this. We can leave this place now."

"No," she replied immediately. "Someone was murdered here, of that I am certain."

"Then we will do our best to find the victim," the professor replied. "We'll start with the bedroom facing the front of the house.

Robert, you and Allen set-up the equipment, while Miss Hill and I set the candles."

The only furniture in the room was a simple wooden bed topped with a torn and stained straw mattress, illuminated by the shaft of moonlight entering through the narrow window. The wooden planks of the floor were worn down, and there were cracks on the plastered walls. Allen had set the camera on a tripod at one end of the room, but cautioned us that the lighting was too low to clearly capture an image. The phonograph, which was used to both record our observations and capture any unusual sounds, sat on top of the wooden chest which we used to transport our equipment. Next to the chest was a kit containing a basic assortment of tools, including a crowbar, hammer and saw.

"It...she is in this room," Dorothy half-whispered to us, her breathing more laboured as she appeared to sway slightly.

I went to her side and offered her my arm to steady herself, which she accepted.

"Thank you, Mr. Evans, I felt light headed for a moment but I've regained my composure now." She took a few steps towards the bed, then shut her eyes and stood silently for several moments, a grave look upon her pale face. "What we seek lies under the bed," she whispered, "beneath the floorboards."

We slid the bed over to the far wall then started to pry the floorboards loose with the aid of a crowbar. The first plank we removed revealed a skull whose forehead had been shattered by a powerful blow.

"God almighty," I murmured, taking a step back, "she really was murdered..."

The room remained silent as Allen and I lifted the remaining floorboards surrounding the body, revealing a woman's skeleton, the tatters of a black dress still clinging to it. But what was truly unnerving was the condition of the corpse's hands. In stark contrast to the white colour of the skeleton's bones, they were pitch-black.

I suddenly felt nauseous and in desperate need of fresh air.

"Forgive me professor, but I am in need of some air." I turned to Dorothy and, noticing her pale complexion, asked, "Perhaps you would like to join me, Miss Hill?"

"She must stay a while longer with me, Robert," came the quick reply from the professor. "I hope you don't mind, Miss Hill, but I need to record your experience using the phonograph, while it is still fresh in your mind."

"Not at all, professor. Please go on ahead, Mr. Evans, and thank you for your offer."

I gave a slight nod then turned and left the room.

Once outside, I took in several deep breaths before looking up at the dimly lit window on the second floor, envisioning the black, murderous hands of Mrs. Burwick. As I stood there, I became aware of a scraping sound, and to my astonishment, realized that one of the bricks below the window was loose and protruding from the wall. I watched in stunned silence as it slid forward and fell to the ground. I took but a single step forward before I froze in horror. A thick, black ooze was escaping from the gap below the window, slowly making its way down the brick facade. A woman's face took shape in the sludge, the mouth wide open as if in agony. Then, with a sickening sound of flesh striking the pavement, the sludge dropped onto the doorstep before sliding off into the small patch of grass next to it, being absorbed immediately into the ground.

It suddenly turned dark as clouds blocked the moonlight. I took a few unsteady steps away from the house until I almost stumbled over the water pump. With a sigh of relief, I pumped the cool water onto my handkerchief, wiping my face and moistening my lips before pressing it to the back of my neck. A moment later, the blessed moonlight made its return.

"Are you alright?" asked the professor as I entered the room, eyeing me with concern.

"Yes, I'm fine now. I just needed to splash some water on my face to revive myself." I did not tell him of my experience, as I myself did not want to believe it.

"Perhaps you could assist Allen with setting up the camera next to the body, so we can begin taking photographs."

I took the tripod from the far wall and positioned it by the feet of the corpse. The moon's rays were falling upon the skeletal hands, and what I saw caused my blood to run cold.

"Professor!" I cried out in alarm.

Everyone gathered around me as I pointed towards the body. There was a gasp from Dorothy as I uttered;

"The hands...the bones are now stark white..."

We met again as a group a fortnight later. The professor was very excited, having prepared a case study on the Burwick House that he was to present to the prestigious Psychical Research Society of Paris in a few days. He was to depart tomorrow and Allen would be accompanying him.

"I have received credible information of another haunting from my journalist friend, located but an hour's distance from the Burwick

House, on a street by the name of Gable's Lane," he announced to the group. "I would be grateful if you and Miss Hill could go and take an initial look at the place while Allen and I are away. If Miss Hill detects a spiritual presence, we can then proceed with a scientific investigation upon my return."

"I'm happy to do so, professor, if Miss Hill agrees."

"I have no objection," replied Dorothy.

"Excellent. You can collect the key from the estate agent Saturday morning. I've arranged to have a carriage at your disposal, but kindly return it no later than four o'clock the same day."

The morning proved chilly as we traveled northward to our destination. I offered my jacket to Dorothy who draped it over her knees.

"You did well to wear gloves today, Mr. Evans. I wish I had been as wise as you."

On the way, she asked many questions about my research on electromagnetism, seeming to be genuinely interested in the subject. At one point, she requested that I bring the carriage to a stop.

"Are you not feeling well?" I inquired.

She remained silent as she looked about slowly with a puzzled expression. "I sense...a presence, similar to that of Burwick House," she eventually replied.

"We are but a half-hour from our destination, perhaps you are sensing a spirit from that location?"

She gave a slight shrug of her shoulders. "Perhaps," she said, unconvincingly. "Please proceed, Mr. Evans. My apologies for the delay."

"Think nothing of it."

The house stood alone off the main road, at the end of a dusty laneway. A tall oak tree crowded one side of the Georgian-style home, the exterior of which showed signs of neglect, with its overgrown hedges and dirty windows. I unlocked the front door for Dorothy, who entered without hesitation. The interior was bright, the late morning sun streaming through the curtainless windows, and the room was well-furnished, although most items were covered by sheets.

Dorothy was a few steps ahead of me when she stopped suddenly, then, after a moment's hesitation, turned slowly to face me.

"Mr. Evens," she said, uneasily. "Please be so kind as to remove your gloves."

Dear Professor Taylor,

April 17, 1888—

As per your request, Miss Hill and I have visited the house on Gable's Lane. I am writing this letter from the tea-table in its parlor room while Miss Hill lies on the sofa across from me.

I have never revealed to you, or to the other members of our group, what I witnessed at the Burwick House when I stepped out for a breath of fresh air, fearing you would all think me mad. What I saw was a black, gelatinous abomination fall from below the second-story window where it was immediately swallowed by the ground. I tried to rid the scene from my mind, but several days later I noticed one of my handkerchiefs was stained black, the very one I used to wipe my face from the water pump at Burwick House. This morning, I awoke to discover my own hands stained black, and most frightening of all, an urge to kill had taken hold of me.

You see, don't you professor, that the foul thing contaminated the earth as it entered the ground, including the water I placed upon my lips by way of my handkerchief. It is inside me, and I am bound to fulfill its dark desire. I have just strangled the kindest and most beautiful creature I have ever known.

I leave for Paris tonight, professor. You will have received this letter the day after my departure. Only you know what I've written here to be true. I hope you have the courage to seek me out and do what must be done. And for God's sake, not a trace of my hands must remain, not even their blackened ashes.

HANDS OF FATE

A Lieutenant Eastman Mystery, 1971

Lieutenant Eastman watched his two children hurriedly make their way towards the amusement rides. His wife was away visiting her ailing mother for the weekend, and it was she who suggested that he take Jeffrey and Michelle to the fall carnival.

"Don't worry," she reassured him, "they're old enough to go on the rides on their own. I know you can't stomach them." She was right.

Just the sight of the spinning amusement rides made him feel queasy.

The children soon disappeared among the bustling crowd, and as he now had a couple of hours to spare, Lieutenant Eastman decided to head over to the food stands for a corn dog and root beer. He regretted his decision a short time later, the food settling in his stomach like a lead weight. He reasoned walking was the best way to aid his digestion, and so strolled along the rows of brightly lit game booths. He tried his luck at a few of the games, eventually winning a small, pink, plush toy of some creature he didn't recognize. "Probably a character from a Saturday morning cartoon," he murmured to himself, staring at the toy with a puzzled frown. A young girl with her mother strolled by, and Lieutenant Eastman took the opportunity to hand the toy over to the girl, who appeared equally baffled as to what kind of animal it was.

"Enjoy," he said with a smile, then turned and walked quickly away in case the child decided to return it, or worse, cry.

Not long after, a palm reading booth caught his attention. It was in the shape of a traditional gypsy wagon, with elaborate carvings and vibrant paintwork. Adjacent to the three wooden steps leading to its interior, a sign read 'Palm Reading, $2.00'. A woman wearing peasant clothes, a headscarf and adorned in necklaces and bracelets sat on the second step, a look of sorrow on her face. With time to spare, he decided to have his fortune told, not because he believed in such nonsense, but because he felt sorry for the woman.

She forced a smile as he approached. "Would you like your palm read?" she asked.

The lieutenant nodded in reply.

She led him inside and told him to have a seat across from her. The interior was small, and not surprisingly, possessed a mystical ambiance, with its heavily draped walls and collection of candles and crystals scattered about.

He placed his open hands on the table, and she began to trace her finger along some of the creases on his palms. She spoke in generalities, uttering phrases like 'you may...it's possible...sometime in your future,' but one comment drew his notice;

"You have a very long lifeline," she began, tracing her finger along a crease that ran from between his thumb and index finger down to the base of his palm, "especially for a policeman."

Surprised, he looked up and asked, "Which line on my palm told you I was a cop?"

"None," she answered with a half-smile. "I know a cop when I see one because I was married to one for ten years."

"I see. You said 'was'—I take it things did not end well."

She shrugged her shoulders. "I'm sure you've heard it all before. At one point my husband started to bring his work home. He became obsessed with a particular cold case. A missing child, I believe. Eventually, he spent more time working on the case than he did with me. He started drinking heavily the last year we were together. One night we argued and he slugged me one. Broke my nose. So, I left." She gave another shrug as she leaned back in her chair, adding, "Sorry, too much information."

"No need to apologize. Sadly, I'm all too familiar with your story." After a moment's silence, the lieutenant asked, "Do you do this full time?"

She gave a soft laugh. "Not a chance. I have a clerical job at a mom-and-pop car dealership. My granny was big on astrology and palm reading, so I learned how to read palms from her. When the carnival comes to town, I work evenings and weekends as 'Madame Fortuna'. Gives me a little extra cash that I send to my daughter in Nevada. She's got two kids to feed."

"Kids are expensive; I have two of my own." He glanced at his watch and added, "Which I promised to meet in five minutes."

Reaching into his wallet, he passed a five-dollar bill across the table to her. "Thank you for the reading. And take care of yourself..." he paused and looked at her enquiringly.

"Janet, the names Janet."

"I'm Lieutenant Eastman. I'll come by next year, Janet, and let you know if any of your predictions panned out."

She smiled. "I'll be here, lieutenant."

On Monday afternoon, a Chevrolet Vega pulled up and parked alongside the curb on Carroll Avenue. The driver, a youthful, blond-haired man, did not bother to feed the parking metre. He waited impatiently, tapping his finger on the steering wheel to the beat of the song playing on the radio. Before long, a second man arrived and looked in through the open passenger window. The driver nodded hello. The second man drew a gun from his pocket and shot him in the head, then walked away.

Detective Samuel Conway was already at the crime scene when the lieutenant arrived.

"What do you have so far, Sam?"

"Not much, Lieutenant. Driver's license identifies the victim as David Brown, twenty-six years of age. Shot in the head from close range with a small caliber pistol, probably at a distance of three or four feet, which places the shooter outside the vehicle."

"So, the shooter just walked up and fired through the passenger window then walked away. Takes some nerve. Any clues to motive?"

"Looks like a drug deal gone bad," replied Detective Conway. "We found Quaaludes and Poppers in his possession, plus a few grams of Cocaine."

"You'd think the shooter would have helped himself to the goods," observed the lieutenant. "Any witnesses?"

"None so far, but we haven't finished canvassing the area."

Lieutenant Eastman looked around before directing his attention to a beauty salon named 'Timeless Beauty' on the opposite side of the street.

"They have an unobstructed view of the crime scene," he pointed out, "I can see clearly into the store interior from here. There are a couple of women sitting on comfortable-looking chairs having a manicure."

"I'll head over and question them," volunteered the detective.

"No need, Sam. I'll take care of it. You follow up with the other officers and see if they tracked down any witnesses."

Though not particularly large, the salon was well furnished with acrylic chairs atop colourful vinyl flooring. The lighting was bright and a few plants hung from the ceiling. Three chairs were evenly spaced along a counter that ran the length of one wall, each facing a large mirror in front of which were arranged blow dryers, flat irons and other styling equipment. Towards the rear of the salon, two women were sitting comfortably in plush chairs receiving manicures.

"May I help you?" inquired the attractive woman behind the counter.

Lieutenant Eastman presented his badge. "I'm sure you've noticed the number of patrol cars across the street. We're canvassing the area for witnesses."

"Witnesses?"

"Yes, I was hoping someone here may have noticed or heard something during the time the crime was committed."

"Crime? I'm not sure what crime you're referring to, but I hadn't noticed anything unusual until a police car with flashing lights stopped across the street. A few minutes later there were several more."

"Before then, did you notice the car that was parked there, a brown Chevrolet Vega?"

"No. Cars come and go all day long on that side of the street. It has metered parking."

"And you didn't hear a bang or sharp 'pop' before the police car arrived?"

"No, I did not. What's this all about, was someone shot?"

"I'm afraid so. I'm sorry, but I'll need to ask the same questions to your staff and customers. It won't take long. By the way, how many people work here?"

"There are five of us, but Cheryl doesn't show up until six, when we get busier servicing our after work clientele. I'm the manager."

The two female employees performing the manicures had their backs to the entrance so they didn't see the car nor did they hear anything unusual. The same was true for the two female customers, who were busy conversing with the staff while their nails were being done. Ms. Baxter, the final employee interviewed by the lieutenant, stated that she had finished styling her client's hair at 3 pm and had seen her out of the salon. She felt quite sure that no brown vehicle was parked across the street then. The lieutenant jotted the point down in his notepad.

"I overheard you tell our manager that someone was shot. Did the person die?" inquired Ms. Baxter.

"I'm afraid so."

"Sad. I guess the person was marked for death."

"That's a curious thing to say, Ms. Baxter"

"I just meant that their time had come. The same as if you cross the street one day and get hit by a car."

"Personally, I always look both ways before crossing, but I get your point—there's no escaping fate."

"No, there isn't"

Before departing, Lieutenant Eastman handed his card to the manager. "Should anyone recall anything further, please have them reach out to me." He noticed a glass bowl on the counter filled with mints, each individually wrapped in bright green foil.

"Do you mind if I take one?"

"Take as many as you wish, Lieutenant."

"Thanks."

Detective Conway was waiting outside the salon when the lieutenant stepped out. He tossed the detective a mint, unwrapped one for himself, then asked, "Any witnesses?"

"None, Lieutenant. How about inside, anyone see anything?"

The lieutenant shook his head. "Nothing more we can do here. Let's go and check out the deceased's address."

The landlady informed them that David Brown had vacated his flat a month earlier, having decided to move in with his girlfriend. They obtained the forwarding address he had left with her, an apartment situated on Linden Street, a short fifteen-minute drive from their current location. When they arrived, the building superintendent let them into the suite as no one answered the buzzer. A woman, dressed in a bathrobe, lay dead on the couch.

"Any idea on the cause of death, doc?" inquired Lieutenant Eastman.

The medical examiner, a short, stocky man with a receding hairline, shook his head. "Can't say. She appears to have been a fit, young woman. No needle marks, nothing to indicate she was a drug user, or at least I won't know for sure until the postmortem examination."

Lieutenant Eastman nodded his head in agreement. "We had a look around the apartment before you arrived. Neat and tidy, no drug paraphernalia, no sign of drugs, not even weed. I wouldn't be surprised if she had no idea her boyfriend dealt in drugs. What about time of death?"

"I'd place it between 10 am and noon," replied the medical examiner, as he bent down for a closer inspection of the woman's hands. The lieutenant looked over his shoulder. He couldn't help but notice the creases on her palms, wondering if Madame Fortuna would have foretold of her death. After a minute, the medical examiner stood up and gestured to the crew to take the body away. He then turned to Lieutenant Eastman, a puzzled expression on his face.

"What's up?" asked the lieutenant.

The medical examiner shrugged his shoulders before answering. "Minor irritation on the tips of some of the fingers. Maybe nothing of importance, but four weeks ago I examined another female body, cause of death undetermined, who also displayed skin irritation around some of her fingers. Similar profile in that the woman was well-groomed, in her thirties, physically fit."

"That is curious. Do me a favour, doc, when you send me the autopsy report, include your previous one as well."

Lieutenant Eastman received the post-mortem results a few days later. The autopsies of both women indicated cardiac arrest as the most probable cause of death with evidence of pulmonary edema noted. "I don't like this," he told himself as he dialed Detective Conway's extension. A minute later, the detective was in his office.

"Help yourself to a cup of coffee, Sam." He did so, then seated himself in one of the dark, vinyl-upholstered chairs facing the desk. The lieutenant handed the autopsy folders to the detective. "Have a look at these. One's the autopsy report for Mr. Brown's girlfriend on Linden Street, who goes by the name of Amanda Miller, the other for a woman who died four weeks earlier."

The detective studied the files for a few minutes. "Probable heart failure, unusual for what appears to be two otherwise healthy females," he observed.

"My feelings exactly, Sam. I need you to spend some time at the vital records office going through the death certificates for the past twelve months. We can narrow the search down to females between the ages of eighteen and forty-five, with the cause of death listed as 'undetermined'."

"Will do, Lieutenant, but it may take a few days."

"Have the new fellow give you a hand...Jimmy is it?"

"James," corrected Detective Conway, "James Campbell."

"Let James know this is a priority, and that I appreciate his understanding."

"I'll let him know. We'll get started this morning."

Detective Conway was back in the lieutenant's office on Friday afternoon. "Nineteen women matching your criteria have passed away this past year," he reported, handing the folder over to Lieutenant Eastman.

The lieutenant took a few minutes to look through the list of names, returned the folder, then rose from his seat and walked over to the large city map that hung on the opposite wall. He motioned for the detective to follow. "Read out each of the addresses while I pin them on the map." When all nineteen locations were marked, the two men stepped back to view the result. A cluster of seven pins confined to a five-block radius caught both men's attention.

"There's no way that's a coincidence," stated the lieutenant gravely. "It has the hallmark of a serial killer."

"It certainly appears so," came the detective's quiet confirmation.

They remained silent for a few minutes, searching for other possible patterns on the map, but none were apparent.

"Of the seven women in the city cluster," began the lieutenant, "who would be the most recent victim, outside of the two women in the autopsy reports on my desk?"

Detective Conway leafed through the death certificates. "That would be...Lisa Hall, who passed away three months ago."

"Her age?"

"She was nineteen."

"Track down the next of kin. Hopefully she was still living at home at the time. Perhaps her parents can tell us something about her movements during her final days."

It turned out that Lisa was not home with her parents the weekend she died, but rather with her friend, Judy Adams, who had an apartment in the city. They spent Saturday shopping and had dinner out before taking in a movie. Judy told the police that Lisa started to feel ill after the movie, and went to bed soon after they got home. Judy was employed at the local diner, and started her shift at 7 am the next day. She didn't check in on Lisa before she left for work as they had planned to have lunch together. When Lisa didn't show up for lunch, Judy got worried and went to her apartment. She found Lisa struggling to breathe, and by the time the ambulance arrived, Lisa had passed away.

The lieutenant nodded sympathetically as Mrs. Hall recounted the events. He asked a few questions but the answers provided little that would help with the investigation. Before leaving, he inquired if they had kept any of her possessions.

"Yes, Lieutenant," replied Mrs. Hall with a half-sad smile, her eyes watering over. "The room is as she left it. We cannot get ourselves to remove her belongings. You are welcome to go upstairs and take a look, if you feel it will help you with your investigation into the cause of my daughter's death. Her room is at the end of the hall."

The room was furnished with a twin bed, neatly made and draped with a brown and yellow patterned bedspread. A tall dresser stood on one wall, with a mirrored vanity table on the opposite side. A desk faced the only window in the room, with textbooks neatly stacked next to the reading lamp. A high-school jacket was draped over the back of the desk chair. The room had been aired out recently and there was no dust on the furniture. With a sigh, the lieutenant wondered how long parents maintain a child's room following a tragedy.

A purse lay next to the vanity table, the contents of which the lieutenant examined. There was only one item that caught his eye, something he had seen recently. "What are the odds?" he asked himself, pocketing the item. Several Polaroids were taped around the border of the vanity mirror; most were of Lisa with her friends at school. He detached one photo and examined it closely. It was a headshot of Lisa, smiling with her head tilted to one side, hands opened wide on either side of her face. Once again, he could not help but hear Madame Fortuna's voice in his head, as if she were reading Lisa's fortune. A strange notion was beginning to formulate in his mind. He slid the photograph into his breast pocket and left the room.

Upon his return to the precinct, he wasted no time in calling Detective Conway into his office.

"Come around to my side of the desk, Sam, and have a look at these photos."

Lieutenant Eastman removed the photograph from his pocket and placed it on the desk.

"Is that the Hall girl?" inquired the detective.

Lieutenant Eastman nodded as he placed two more photographs next to the first, one from each of the autopsy folders. He then placed his right hand, palm-up, at the end of the row of photographs.

"I want you to compare the palms of each of the women in these photos with that of my own."

The detective did so, but after a minute looked up at the lieutenant and shook his head in the negative.

"Focus on the creases of the palm," the lieutenant added.

"I think I see what you're getting at," came the response after a few moments, as he tapped his finger on one of the photographs, "but I don't understand what this has to do with any of the deaths."

"It's too far-fetched for an explanation at this point," replied the lieutenant as he gathered the photographs. "But you can help me get the proof I need by paying a visit to the beauty salon across the road from last week's shooting, 'Timeless Beauty' I believe it was called. Get a hold of their appointment calendar. Make up some excuse as to why we need it, as I don't want anyone to think we suspect something's going on there. Also, get one of our photographers to take photos of the manager and the four employees that work there. Ask him to shoot from across the road when they show up for work as I don't want them to know they're being photographed."

"I'll see to it this afternoon, Lieutenant. But what makes you suspect the beauty salon, aside from the fact that it's located within the five block radius of interest?"

From his pocket, Lieutenant Eastman took the small object he had removed from the girl's purse earlier that day and tossed it to Detective Conway. It was a mint wrapped in bright green foil.

"Lieutenant," began the detective, shutting the door to the phone booth, "it turns out that the beauty salon does not keep a bound appointment book, but instead uses a monthly calendar pad with tear-off sheets. Unfortunately, they throw away each sheet after the month ends." On the other end of the receiver, he heard the lieutenant give a long sigh before replying, "Thanks for trying, Sam."

"Not so fast, Lieutenant. As we're only two days into August, I decided to look through their trash out back and guess what I found?"

"Tell me it was the calendar sheet for July."

"Bingo. And guess who had their nails done a week ago, on the day before they died?"

"The girlfriend of the deceased drug dealer, Amanda Miller"

"Right again, Lieutenant."

"Great work, Sam. Now what about the photography, is everything set up?"

"All good. The photographer will be there tomorrow morning. He's going to shoot from a car parked nearby. Said he'll have the photos to you by that afternoon. Lieutenant, if you don't mind my asking, who do you plan to show them to?"

"Madame Fortuna."

"Back so soon, Lieutenant?"

The lieutenant gave her a smile before answering. "Hello, Janet. I'm hoping you can help me with a case I'm working on."

"A case?" she said in surprise. "Of course, Lieutenant, but I can't foretell where criminals disappear to after they commit a crime."

"That's OK," he answered with a chuckle, "I'm not here for psychic detective work, I just need you to look through a few photographs. I was hoping you might recognize one as a former customer."

"In that case, c'mon in and have a seat."

"This one," said Madame Fortuna, placing her finger on one of the five photographs the lieutenant had arranged on the table before sliding it towards him.

"You're sure?"

"Absolutely, Lieutenant. She took my reading very seriously. Started to tell me her entire life story, husband died in a car accident, she had a breakdown and had to leave her work, and so on. It wasn't easy getting her to leave. I had other customers waiting."

"Did she tell you where she worked?"

"She did, but I don't remember the name of the company. I believe it was for a chemical or pharmaceutical company. After her breakdown a friend got her a low-stress job at a beauty salon. She gave me a card and said she'd give me a free manicure. And before you ask, I'm sorry but I didn't keep the card."

"There's no need to apologize," Lieutenant Eastman replied, his tone courteous, "you've been a great help."

He was about to leave when he turned to her and asked, "By the way, can I see your palm?"

She held it up for him to see.

"It was a wise choice not to take her up on the free manicure. You can consider yourself extremely fortunate."

An undercover police woman, smartly dressed in a floral-print skirt paired with a white button-down blouse and brown knee-high boots, walked confidently into the Timeless Beauty salon on a sunny Wednesday morning.

The woman behind the counter glanced down at the appointment calendar before greeting her, "Good morning. You must be Amy."

"That's right. I have an appointment for a manicure with Ms. Baxter."

"She'll be right with you. In the meantime, have a seat at one of the tables at the back. Did you have a particular colour in mind?"

"Yes, I did. I think I'll go with a green, preferably avocado green if you have it."

"We certainly do. I'll get it for you and bring it over."

A minute or two later, a tall, slender woman entered from the curtained doorway at the rear of the salon. She smiled as she sat down in front of Amy and introduced herself as Ms. Baxter.

"I see you've already chosen a lovely colour. Let's have a look at your nails before we begin."

Amy held out her hands. "Very nice," commented Ms. Baxter, tracing the tip of her finger across a few of her finger nails. "Now let's have a quick peek at the underside of the nails."

Amy turned her hands palm upwards.

Ms. Baxter stared at them for a few moments before looking up at Amy and saying, "I've left my nail polish remover in the back. I'll see if we have a new bottle of green nail polish while I'm there, as there may not be enough in this bottle. While I'm gone, you can soak your fingertips in this bowl of warm water to help soften the cuticles."

In the back room, Ms. Baxter slipped on a pair of disposable gloves before reaching into her large canvas tote bag to remove a bottle of nail polish remover and an eyeglass case, from which she took out a syringe.

She returned a couple of minutes later, carrying both nail polish and nail polish remover.

"Now," she said, sitting herself down once again in front of Amy, "let's dry your fingertips before I remove your clear polish."

Amy withdrew her hands and placed them on her lap. "I'm afraid you won't get that opportunity, Ms. Baxter."

Detective Conway emerged from behind the curtained doorway. He charged Ms. Baxter with seven counts of murder and escorted her out through the back exit where a police cruiser was waiting to take her to the precinct.

By eight that evening both men were in the lieutenant's office, their ties loosened and the toll of a long day visible on their weary faces. Two cups of tepid coffee sat on the desk.

"You know, Sam," the lieutenant thought out loud, "chance has played a role in just about every aspect of this case."

"I can see that," replied the detective after a brief reflection. "The victim of a car shooting dies in front of a beauty salon whose girlfriend had her nails done at that very spot by a serial killer the day before."

"Sounds pretty remarkable when you put it like that. By the way, was the shooting homicide solved?"

"Yes, Mr. Brown was a drug dealer who tried to muscle his way into a bike gang's turf. They settled the issue quickly with a bullet to his head. We have a warrant out for the shooter's arrest. He has a long rap sheet and it won't be long before we nab him."

"Good work, Sam."

"Thanks, Lieutenant." Redirecting the conversation back to the serial murders, the detective asked, "Whatever made you focus in on the victim's palms as the key to the murders?"

"It was the coroner who drew my attention to the victim's hands. He found signs of irritation on the tips of the fingers. As he examined the finger tips, I focused on the palms, especially the creases of the palms, no doubt because I had had my own palm read recently. It was uncanny, as if Janet's...that is, Madame Fortuna's voice was in the back of my mind as I looked at the victim's palms. When I eventually came across Lisa Hall's photo, it dawned on me that the photos of all three victims had one thing in common—a short lifeline on their palms. At that point I began to suspect that the killer was targeting people with a short lifeline. Finding the mint from the beauty salon in Linda's purse strengthened my belief. Who better to unknowingly examine the victim's palms and administer poison than a manicurist? When I reviewed the notes I took at the beauty salon, I was struck by a curious phrase Ms. Baxter used when commenting on the shooting victim, that he was 'marked for death'. Perhaps she had marked certain customers for death, those with a short lifeline. But it was not until Madame Fortuna's identification of Ms. Baxter as a past customer that I was sure we were onto the killer. And by the way, good job finding a policewoman with a short lifeline for the undercover work. I won't dare ask how many palms you had to inspect."

"Way too many," replied the detective. "I'm sure every precinct I went to now thinks I have a palm fetish."

"I'm sure it will soon be forgotten," the lieutenant remarked with a laugh.

"But how about the poison?" continued the detective. "Has the lab determined what type she was administering?"

"Preliminary results suggest that her bottle of nail polish remover was a potent solution of parathion, a highly toxic pesticide, spiked with lavender extract to mask the odour. As she was removing the victim's old nail polish, she was also administrating poison to their fingertips and nails at the same time. Naturally, she wore disposable gloves during this procedure, a common practice among manicurists. In addition to parathion, we also found a syringe and a solution of potassium cyanide in an eyeglass case in her handbag, which she would inject into the bottle of nail polish when she went to get a 'new' bottle for the client. Once applied, the cyanide would seep through the victim's nails and into their fingertips. I'm sure we can trace the poisons to the chemical companies she worked for."

"Must have been a nasty way to die," ventured the detective.

"It most certainly was. The victim would start feeling ill a few hours later, try to sleep it off, but find themselves on death's doorstep by the morning."

"Clearly the woman must be insane," concluded the detective. "What did the psychologist have to say?"

"He only had ten minutes with her, but he believes Ms. Baxter is suffering from a delusional disorder, that she believes she has a divine right to end a life, as dictated by the victim's short lifeline. In her eyes, she was just fulfilling the destiny set out for them in their palms."

"Sad that seven people lost their lives because of her insane conviction."

"It most certainly is, Sam."

Both men stifled a yawn as they reached for their coffees, each grimacing after taking a sip.

"God, that's horrible. I think the department is trying to poison us!"

The lieutenant gave a soft chuckle. "It won't work, Sam. What they don't know is that we both have long lifelines."

SCARECROW

Sevier County, Tennessee, 1923

Jake stood just inside the barn door, watching the menacing dark clouds draw nearer. A ray of sunlight broke through and illuminated the crooked frame of a scarecrow near the centre of the corn field. The shaft of light gave it a particularly sinister appearance, starkly outlined against the threatening sky, its long, torn cape flapping wildly in the wind, accompanied by the sibilant whispers of the corn stalks brushing against one another.

Coming down the dirt lane next to the field, Earl's truck, a Model T he used for delivering moonshine, came to a stop beside the barn.

"Looks like we're in for some nasty weather," Earl said, stepping out of the vehicle and hastily making his way toward Jake.

Looking up at the leaden sky, Jake replied, "The clouds are moving fast, so I think the worst of it will move past quickly"

"Let's hope so," Earl added, joining Jake inside the barn, the two men staring out into the field. "Never seen that old scarecrow look so alive. Kinda gives me the creeps."

As they watched it in the distance, the sky suddenly lit up as a bolt of lightning struck the field, setting the scarecrow on fire. "Damn, will you look at that!" exclaimed Earl. Thunder rumbled overhead, unleashing a torrential downpour that prevented the men from leaving the barn. They felt a wave of relief when the rainfall quickly extinguished the flames, and the worst of the storm lifted a short time later, just as Jake had anticipated.

"Let's go check on the damage," Jake said. "And grab that shovel next to you on the way out."

There was surprisingly little damage to the corn stalks surrounding the scarecrow, perhaps a few dozen plants flattened and charred. Much more alarming was that the frame of the scarecrow was still standing, with a human skull now perched where a straw head had previously been.

"Is that..." Earl began, somewhat hesitantly, "is that what I think it is?"

Jake nodded his head in reply. "Must've been hiding under the straw head all these years." He took the shovel from Earl and used the end of its handle to slide the skull off the frame, where it dropped onto the damp earth below. He bent down for a closer look.

"Maybe we should...call the cops," Earl hesitated.

"Don't even think it!" Jake exclaimed as he rose and cast a stern look at Earl. "If they start poking their noses around these parts and find our distillery we're done for. Best thing to do now is bury the damn thing and put up a new scarecrow. Don't tell nothing to no one, either."

"You know I'd never do that, Jake," Earl replied, removing his hat and running his fingers through his thinning hair. It suddenly occurred to him to ask, "How come the frame didn't burn?"

Jake tapped the frame with the shovel before answering, "Metal tube." He glanced back at Earl, nodding for him to come over. "Give me a hand to pull it out of the ground."

The frame didn't budge despite several vigorous attempts to free it.

"Must be anchored to something in the ground," Jake said, catching his breath. "Pass me the shovel, Earl."

He dug down a foot before handing the shovel back to Earl. They took turns digging until Jake struck something several feet down. Scraping away the earth above it, he realized it was a wooden chest, roughly two by three feet in length. "Looks like the rod is bolted to the back side of the chest. Let's get it to the surface for a better look."

It was not very heavy, and when Jake used the shovel to force the padlock open, they discovered the reason why. Inside was a human skeleton, fragments of decayed clothing still clinging to its bones. Its head was missing.

They stared silently at the scattered bones, a vague feeling of unease gaining on them when the sudden call of a crow circling overhead caused them to look up unexpectedly.

"I don't like this, Jake," Earl began nervously, "Crows have never attacked your crops. This is a bad omen. Let's put it back where it was and forget we ever found it."

Jake remained silent, mulling over what to do next. After a few moments, he scooped up the skull with the shovel and placed it inside the chest before dropping the lid shut.

"Help me remove the metal tube and then we'll take the chest to the barn. Tomorrow morning we'll bury it up in the hills, next to Wally's abandoned distillery. No one will ever find it there. I don't want it anywhere near my farm. If whoever did this is still around and decides to start a rumour about a dead body in my field, it could cause a lot of trouble for me."

"Sure, Jake. That's what we'll do. And the sooner the better. I'm not going to sleep easy until that thing is back in the ground. Who do you think he was?"

Jake shrugged his shoulders. "Don't know. Folks have been known to go missing around these parts in the past. Guess someone thought this was a good spot to hide a body."

Both men stood eyeing the chest curiously before Earl remarked, "Maybe it's a *padre*."

Jake shot him a dubious look. "A *padre*? What the hell is that?"

"Beat's me," admitted Earl, "but old man Liam says every scarecrow in these parts has one. Says their job is to guard the scarecrows, make sure they're always standing in the fields, so the crows don't come."

Jake dismissed Earl's gossip with a wave of the hand. "Old man Liam is a lazy drunk and as crazy as a coot. Anyway, don't matter who it is. Let's get this chest to the barn. Tomorrow morning we'll load it onto your truck and be on our way to bury it."

Each of them grabbed a handle on opposite sides and made their way through the corn field towards the barn. They were almost clear of the field when they heard a vehicle approaching. "Leave the chest here," Jake whispered across to Earl, before they continued on to see who it was.

Curtis, whose family spanned three generations of farmers, had parked his truck next to Earl's. He waved when he spotted the men leaving the field.

"What the devil does he want," murmured Jake as Curtis made his way over to them. When he was within earshot, Jake said, "Hello Curtis, good to see you. What brings you out here this afternoon?"

"Just being neighbourly. Been going around to most of the farms in the area to see if the storm caused any damage. I'd help in any way I can if—" He stopped abruptly, a look of concern crossing his broad face as he took a couple of steps to one side of Jake and pointed to the white wooden fence that bordered part of the crop, where a few crows were now perched.

"Crows!" he said in astonishment. His eyes widened further as he added in disbelief, "The scarecrow...gone! Why'd you do that for, Jake?"

Jake shot a sideways glance at Earl before answering, "I didn't. Lightning struck it."

"Oh, that was bad luck. But the frame is made of metal, it should still be standing."

Jake looked at him suspiciously before answering. "Wind must have knocked it over. Why are you so worried about my scarecrow, anyway?"

"Ain't a farm within a hundred miles of here that hasn't had a scarecrow standing every day of the year since they got started, and that's a fact. If there's no scarecrow, then the crows come, like they've started to do on your farm. Take my advice, Jake, best if you get that scarecrow back up today...put everything back just like it was before the lightning struck. No use messing with what's been shown to be tried and true, is there?"

"My farm, I do as I like," Jake replied defensively. "But you needn't worry yourself, Curtis, I plan to put up a new scarecrow. Tomorrow is soon enough...or the day after."

"Tomorrow..." Curtis repeated softly, before adding, "As you say, you can do as you want." He turned and started towards his truck before stopping to address Jake once more. "My great granddaddy used to say that a scarecrow is made to frighten, and to do so, to really frighten, it must know *evil*. I wouldn't give it that chance." He nodded goodbye and once again turned to leave.

"What'd he mean by that?" Earl asked in alarm.

"Don't know, but I wouldn't be surprised if he or one of his kin buried the body under the scarecrow. Don't matter now, anyway. As of tomorrow, it'll be gone. If he comes snooping around or has the law come around, there won't be any sign of a body."

They went back to collect the chest, hiding it in one of the shadowy corners of the barn.

Earl thought it wise to go and check out the abandoned distillery before heading home, just to make sure there were no signs that someone had visited the place recently. If everything looked undisturbed, he could scout out the area for a spot to bury the chest.

The rugged country lane that secretly snaked its way up the forested mountain was muddy with the day's morning rain. As he approached a steep bend, something slammed into his windshield. It was a crow, its bloody carcass piercing the glass. "Christ!" Earl cursed, hitting the brakes. The vehicle swerved on the wet earth, its back tire sliding off the road's edge, pulling the rear of the truck with it. Earl slammed his foot onto the accelerator as the truck continued to drift over the edge, but it was already too late. It overturned onto its roof as it plunged down the steep valley, crushing Earl to death as it did so.

The night felt perfectly stifling as Jake lay in bed, the humidity from the day's rain making it impossible to find any comfort. The faint sound of a door creaking drifted in through his open window. He sat up immediately and waited, listening. There it was again, the sound of the barn door being opened. He slipped into his overalls before lighting the kerosene lantern and making his way down the steps and out the back door towards the barn. He took the ax that was resting against the wood-pile as he approached the barn's entrance. The door was slightly ajar. He slowly swung it open with his foot, holding the lantern out in front as he scanned the interior. A shuffling sound came from the dark corner that hid the chest. A faint smile of satisfaction crossed Jake's lips as he took a few steps forward and declared, "C'mon out, Curtis. I've caught you red-handed. I knew you had something to do with that chest."

The shuffling noise drew nearer, but he couldn't make out anyone approaching. Jake set the lantern down on the ground and gripped the ax tightly with both hands. *Damn bastard better not try to ambush me, or by God it will be his head on the scarecrow!*

He took another cautious step forward and then stopped suddenly. The outline of a dark figure was now visible, slowly shuffling towards him. When it finally stepped within the circle of light, Jake cried out in horror.

The skeleton was covered in crows, scores of them, piled on top of one another. Beaks were protruding from the skull's eye sockets and dozens of tiny black eyes gleamed from within its rib cage. There was a brief moment of complete stillness, and then they attacked. Tearing at Jake's flesh, pecking at his eyes and nose, several trying to rip out his tongue. He dropped the ax and fell to his knees as he struggled to tear the birds free from his face, crushing the heads of those that entered his mouth with his teeth. But the birds continued their relentless assault, stripping the flesh from his hands until he could no longer pry the crows from his face.

As suddenly as the attack started, it stopped. Bird carcasses and blood-stained feathers surrounded his kneeling, battered body. The shuffling sound of skeletal feet resumed and came to a stop directly before him. Jake lifted his gaze, and through the bloody slits of his swollen eyes, he caught the flash of an ax blade descending.

A truck makes its way up a dirt lane the following morning and parks next to Jake's barn. Curtis steps out and walks to the rear of the truck, where he removes a placard along with a hammer and a few nails that he drops into his pocket. He makes his way to the edge of the field and looks out at the scarecrow that once again occupies its original location, the straw head stained a deep crimson around the neck. Nodding his head sadly, Curtis utters, "I warned you, Jake...that I did. You should've listened..." Lowering himself to one knee, he positions the FOR SALE sign up against the white wooden fence, then nails it into place.

THE DEATH GOD

Honduras, 1912

I drew up the shade from the narrow window that looked out onto the noisy street below. The sun was beginning to set, and there was a slight breeze, but neither offered relief from the uncomfortable heat in the room. Gordon arrived as I stood with my back facing the door.

"Hello, Cathers," he said pleasantly, "Nice of you to invite me up for a drink."

"Not at all," I replied as I turned and motioned for him to take a seat at one of the chairs opposite my desk.

"Good Lord, man," he exclaimed upon seeing my left arm in a sling. "What the devil happened to you?"

"An unfortunate accident. I'll tell you about it after we've had our drinks." A tray with glasses and a bottle of scotch sat on my desk. I poured each of us a stiff drink before taking my seat.

Gordon took a long sip of his scotch, set the half-empty glass on my desk, and after a moment's pause broke out suddenly;

"Dash it all, Cathers, I was as surprised as you were when the Geographic Society chose me to lead the excavation of the Copan earth mounds. Everyone knows you're the expert when it comes to Aztec ruins."

I let an uncomfortable silence fall upon the room before I answered. "My ancestry goes back many generations in this country, and I have made it my life's work to explore its ruins for over forty years. I guess the learned men of the society felt the task was better suited for a younger, more ambitious explorer."

"Perhaps that is so," Gordon replied softly.

"No matter," I said, with a wave of my hand. "What's done is done. The reason I've asked you here is to show you an artifact I discovered at an excavation I've been conducting for the past two years. It is a pet project of mine. I've told no one about it until now." I reached into the bottom drawer and carefully withdrew a small skeletal figure approximately four inches in height, carved entirely from crystal, and placed it upon the desk. I could see Gordon's eyes widen as he stared at the figure, speechless, his cheeks reddening slightly with excitement.

"But this...this is unbelievable," he stammered, looking up at me.

"It is exceptional, is it not?" I agreed.

"The death god, *Mictlantecuhtli*, exquisitely carved in solid crystal. My God, Cathers, this is the most significant find in years. I recall Maxwell discovering a crystal skull back in '88, but nothing of this calibre. Where did you find it?" he asked eagerly.

I smiled but did not answer his question, instead directing his attention to a detail etched into the figure. "Look here, Gordon," I said, pointing to a small channel that ran down the back of the figure to a small reservoir at its base.

Gordon leaned forward and carefully ran his finger along the length of the channel. "Curious. Any idea what it's for?"

"Unfortunately, I know exactly why it's there." I set the figure to one side and refilled our glasses. "I am going to tell you how I injured my arm, Gordon. You may have trouble believing what I am about to recount to you, but I assure you, it is the truth." I finished my scotch and leaned back in my chair before continuing;

"As I've mentioned, my ancestry goes back many generations, during which time my ancestors recorded the stories and folklore they encountered. I am now the owner of this vast collection of knowledge. Since childhood, I've been fascinated with the stories concerning *Mictlantecuhtli*, ruler of the underworld. One tale in particular described how the god could be summoned, a ceremony involving a small crystalline statue, the one you see before you now. Of course, the use of hallucinogens was necessary—in this case, *tlililtzin*, a brew of morning glory seeds. After drinking the brew, one slit one's thumb, allowing the blood to drip onto the statue, where it would run down the groove and pool in the reservoir carved into its base, calling forth *Mictlantecuhtli*.

"I performed the ceremony as described, and after a few minutes the room appeared to darken and a figure took shape a few feet in front of me. Naturally, I was aware that I was under the influence of a hallucinogenic, but I was not prepared for how real and fearsome the apparition appeared, with its skull head adorned with an elaborate feathered headdress and a skeletal body clad in traditional Aztec garments. He also brandished a large obsidian knife. I was so in awe of its appearance that I reached out to touch it, and as I did so, this happened." I gave my sling a tap.

"I see, you fell forward as you reached out to touch the hallucination," Gordon volunteered.

"Can a hallucination do this?" I said gravely, as I withdrew my arm from the sling and pointed its bandaged stump directly at him. The sight gave Gordon such a start that his chair shot back an inch as he gasped;

"Your...hand—"

"Severed," I interjected. "As I reached out to touch the 'hallucination', it gave a quick strike with its knife, cutting my hand clean off. I fell on my knees, screaming in agony. Thank God the window was open, and I was heard by a couple of passers-by who came to my rescue. I lost consciousness soon after their arrival, but the doctor later informed me that my severed hand was found four feet from where I lay."

Gordon removed a handkerchief from his pocket, wiping the perspiration from his brow. "I am at a complete loss for words," he said. "Your tale is almost too fantastic to believe, and yet..."

"And yet my arm has no hand," I added. "I plan to return this cursed relic back where it came from and seal the cave along with the other artifacts."

"Other artifacts?"

"Yes, there are other artifacts, most depicting *Mictlantecuhtli*, but there is also his wife, *Mictecacihuatl*, the so-called 'Lady of the Dead', and a few lesser gods, such as *Xolotl*. It's an evil place; one can sense it immediately upon entering. I believe it was deliberately sealed long ago in hope that it would never again be discovered."

"But Cathers, you can't be serious! The cave is an extraordinary find, and if there are other pieces like the one you have here—"

"They would make the archaeologist who discovered them world famous, perhaps even wealthy. Yes, Gordon, I realize that, but it's not worth the risk. My ancestor's documents make reference to some terrible scenarios, almost apocalyptic in nature, if one were to amass the relics in that cave. You see, I am not the only one with such knowledge. There are others whose ancestry stretches back further than mine. Others, who may not think twice about using such power."

Disappointment was written all over Gordon's face as he leaned back in his chair, nodding his head slowly. "I would have a difficult time believing in such a doomsday scenario if it where not for your experience," he said in an even tone. "It is an unfortunate situation, but I can tell you've made up your mind. When do you plan to seal the entrance?"

"Tonight. I will leave here around eight. The site is an hour north of here. Fortunately, the wooden frame supporting the entrance is not very secure, so one swift kick to the base of the support beam will cause the entrance to collapse. Even with one hand, I should be able to complete the task quickly."

"I imagine you will. Thank you for the drink, Cathers. I can see my own way out."

I arrived at the site around nine that evening. I lit the kerosene lamp and swung the kit bag containing the crystal figure over my shoulder before making my way towards the cave's opening. Inside, I placed the figure on a large, flat rock located a short distance from the cave's entrance, then seated myself on a second rock a few feet across from it. I set the lantern on the ground and waited.

A quarter of an hour later, a few small pebbles tumbled into the cave.

"You can come in, Gordon," I shouted towards the entrance. "I've been expecting you."

A few moments later the beam of a flashlight was directed towards me as Gordon entered the cave.

"Do you mind pointing that away from my face, I can't see a thing."

He did as I asked.

"Thank you, and don't look so surprised—I knew you would follow me. Not that I blame you. If our roles were reversed I'd do the same." I took up my lantern and pointed it in the direction of the crystal figure. "It's over there, across from where I'm standing, on a large rock. If you look around a bit you may find other artifacts as well."

"Thank you. Cathers. I won't forget this."

"I'm sure you won't." I murmured

I walked over to the entrance, turning to face Gordon once I was standing just beyond it. "Gordon," I said, "I should add that the crystal figure you are marveling at is a fake. I had a local artisan create it. It took him six months to prefect, truly a beautiful work of craftsmanship. As to why I did so, it was critical that I convinced you of its authenticity, especially its 'mystical' properties, or else you would not have come here tonight. So, I fabricated the tale of my ancestor's ancient knowledge, and as the ultimate proof that their writings could conjure forth *Mictlantecuhtli*, I severed my own hand."

"You did...what?" he exclaimed.

"That's right, I cut-off my own hand. Come now, we both know the society made a grave error in selecting you for the Copan excavation. But if you were to meet with a fatal accident while exploring a site I mentioned to you in passing, then naturally I would be your replacement. I would lead what should have always been my responsibility. That is why I lured you here. There is no death god in this cave, only death. Your death, Gordon.

He hurled the crystal figure at me as he charged towards me, but his fate was already sealed. One sharp kick to the wooden frame supporting the overhead rocks caused it to collapse, the rocks crashing down, sealing the entrance shut.

How ironic, I thought to myself as I returned to my vehicle, *that this cave really was a site for human sacrifices to the death god Mictlantecuhtli. I'm sure he'll be pleased to have an offering after all these centuries.*

The thought pleased me immensely, and I whistled merrily for much of the drive home.

THE BARN

Western Hampshire, UK, 1937

The train slowed down as it rounded the bend, eventually coming to a stop at a railway station a few minutes later. I had just stepped onto the narrow platform with my luggage when the train began to pull away. A man, middle-aged, smartly dressed in a tweed jacket, woolen breeches and Wellington boots, approached me from the far side of the platform.

"Good afternoon," he greeted me with a firm handshake, "you must be Mr. Davis."

"Yes, that's right," I replied with a nod.

"I'm Richard Johnson, Lord Johnson's nephew. I have a car waiting for us outside the station. Do you only have the one bag?"

He stepped forward but I caught up my suitcase before he could reach for it. "No need, thank you. It's quite light."

"This way then," he said, pointing in the direction from which he came.

The driver was waiting for us beside a nicely polished, stately looking vehicle. Richard could tell I was admiring it as we drew closer.

"It's a Wolseley Super-Six," he commented. "Not in the same class as a Rolls, but still respectable. Uncle has become more prudent with his expenditures, considering the family fortune isn't what it once was. I guess that's why you're here."

I gave him a questioning look and said, "I'm not entirely sure what you mean. I was asked by the university to catalogue your uncle's library. I understand it has a number of rare volumes."

"It most certainly does, and my uncle is eager to sell them. That's why you're here. The university has expressed interest in purchasing some of his collection."

"I see..." I replied, somewhat surprised by this news. "Then I shall make sure to do a thorough job of it during my time here."

"I'm sure you will," Richard replied with a friendly smile, gesturing with his arm out towards the open passenger door. I stepped inside, grateful for the comfortable seating after the long train journey.

It was a short thirty-minute drive to the Johnson estate. I was shown to my room shortly after our arrival, then served a cold lunch consisting of ox tongue, pickled vegetables, and salad before being taken to the library.

The oak-panel room was large and shelved from floor to ceiling, with a pair of bookcase ladders allowing access to the higher shelves, which I estimated to be twelve or more feet in height. A decorative area rug with a floral motif covered much of the floor, with several chairs and side tables artfully arranged throughout the room. A stone fireplace intricately carved with vines and different woodland creatures, some of a mythological origin, stood opposite the room entrance. Seated at one of the chairs next to the fireplace was a young woman, fair skinned with pale green eyes and auburn hair, who looked up from the book she was reading as I came into the room. She gave me a bright smile as she stood up, placing her book on the chair before coming to greet me.

"You must be Mr. Davis," she said in a pleasant voice. "I'm Barbara. My brother Richard said I should be expecting you." We shook hands, after which she added, "I understand you're here to catalogue my uncle's library."

"Yes, I am. And please, call me William."

She smiled in reply, then said, "As you can see, William, uncle is quite a collector. It may take you several weeks to catalogue them all."

"I'm here only for a week at most, after which I will be on vacation, a leisurely trip through Dorset, Somerset and western Hampshire. You see, when the university learned of my travel plans, they asked if I wouldn't mind taking a small detour here and delaying my trip by a week, as your uncle's estate borders close to Dorset."

"That was very accommodating of you," she commented. "As you only have a week, you may want to begin cataloguing the older, rarer editions. Most are situated on the shelf to the right of the bay window."

"Thank you for letting me know."

She gave me another smile, wished me luck with my work, then excused herself and left the room.

A lovely woman, I thought to myself as I set my pencils and notebook down on the table beside me. I wandered about the room, occasionally removing a volume from the shelf for closer inspection. When I walked past the fireplace, I noticed the book Barbara was reading upon my arrival was left on the chair, face

down, still open at the spot she was last reading. It was entitled *Bibliography of Greek Myth in
English Poetry*. I refrained from picking up and
examining the book, feeling it would be an un-
just trespass on her privacy. Instead, I headed
towards the shelf by the bay window, where I
would begin my work.

There was a knock at the door around five
o'clock and Barbara entered carrying a tray of
tea and biscuits. "I thought you could use a bit
of refreshment," she said, setting the tray on a
nearby table.

"Indeed," I replied, holding back a yawn. "I
was up at the crack of dawn. I'm beginning to
feel the effects."

"What you need is some fresh air," she suggested. "After your tea, perhaps you would like
to explore the grounds a bit before getting
back to your work. There is a lovely path that
runs through our woods at the back of the estate that leads to the top of a hill, offering a decent view of the surrounding area."

"I will take your advice. The outdoor air will
help clear my mind, and I still feel cramped

from riding on the infernal train for so many hours."

She stayed with me while I had my tea, recounting a bit about her family history and the town itself, which relies heavily on agriculture, wheat and barley being the main crops, and on farming, including raising cattle, sheep, and pigs. After tea, she accompanied me as far as the wood path, then reminded me that dinner was at eight-thirty before returning to the house.

From my vantage point at the top of the hill I looked down at the tranquil landscape. Stone and thatch roof farms, interspersed between patches of woodlands, spotted the landscape. After taking in the fresh air for several minutes, I was about to make my way back when a barn, partially hidden by a large ash tree, drew my attention. It was relatively small, constructed of wood, and had the iconic sloped roofs typical of a gable barn. On one side there was a second sloped roof that extended from the base of the main roof, creating a sheltered area for farm equipment. At the top of the barn was a cupola for ventilation, and to my astonishment, there were two children trying to peer into the barn through the openings between the slats of the cupola.

What the devil are they up to? I asked myself.

I made my way down the hill and towards the barn. "You two!" I exclaimed when I was a short distance away, "Get down from there before one of you slips and breaks his neck!" As soon as the words left my mouth I regretted having said them. I gave the children such a start that I was sure they were going to lose their grip on the cupola and come tumbling down the roof. Thankfully, it did not happen. They slid down the roof to the second, lower roof, and from there leaped a short distance onto haystacks leaning against the shelter.

"That was a very foolish thing to do," I scolded the children, whom I judged to be no more than ten years old, as I made my way towards them. "What in heaven's name made you climb up the roof?"

"We wanted to see the baby animals play," answered the shorter of the two.

"And see if we could spot Pam playing the flute," put in the other eagerly.

"Nonsense, why not enter through the barn doors?" I asked in a calmer voice.

The children looked at me as if I were daft before the taller boy responded, "They're locked. No one can go in when the animals play. Everyone knows that."

"Well I, for one, do not. Now, go on home, and if I catch either one of you on that roof again, I'll inform the local constable."

They turned and ran off towards a stream that flowed through a gentle sloping valley opposite the barn.

"Little rascals," I murmured, "no common sense whatever. Mind you, I was probably getting into similar mischief at their age." The thought brought a smile to my face as I headed back to the manor.

Richard and Lord Johnson had left for a hunting excursion earlier that afternoon, so it was only Barbara and me for dinner. We had a pleasant conversation on a number of topics, and it was when she was telling me about her travels as a child that I suddenly remembered my earlier encounter with the boys.

"I came across a couple of lads today trying to peek into a barn by way of its cupola. Obviously I told them to get down and never do such a dangerous thing again. They told me they wanted to see 'the baby animals play'. Do you think they were telling the truth?"

"Sounds like you encountered the Smith boys, and yes, they were telling the truth. It's important that young animals play, so a few times a week we lock them together into the barn with their toys and let them enjoy themselves."

"Toys?" I asked in surprise.

"Sounds odd but young animals enjoy playing with objects that they can knock about. We have hay bundles, pumpkins, tree branches, even a big rubber ball."

"And what about music? The boys said someone played a flute in the barn. Pam, I believe they said her name was."

"Music?" she said with a soft chuckle, "Well, I don't know about that, but I'm sure the animals wouldn't mind if someone did play them a tune."

Just then the clock in the hallway chimed ten. "Good Lord, is that really the time?" I asked, astonished. "I'll have to excuse myself as I head back to the library. At this rate the university will be none too pleased with my progress."

"I won't keep you a moment longer," she said with a smile. "Thank you for your company tonight. I hope you'll join me for breakfast tomorrow."

The next day was much like the first. I met Barbara for a light breakfast and again for tea, then took an afternoon stroll to the top of the hill. The boys I encountered the previous day were nowhere to be seen as I made my way down to the barn. I walked around to the front but found the barn doors barred and padlocked. I peered through the narrow opening between the two doors but could discern little. Dim shafts of sunlight made their way through the wooden slats of the barn walls, illuminating small hay particles floating in the air. I suddenly took a quick step back in alarm as a dark shadow obstructed my view.

"What the devil was that?" I asked out loud, before carefully stepping forward once more to look through the opening.

This time I could make out a large ball rolling across the floor, chased by a calf, followed by the bleating of a lamb. "Good heavens, there really are animals playing in there!" I laughed out loud as I turned and started my walk back to the house. On the way, I thought I could make out a faint, plaintive melody, as if played on a flute. I stopped to listen, but there was only the sound of the wind rustling the leaves.

At dinner, I told Barbara that I had glimpsed the animals playing in the barn that afternoon, and wondered why the barn doors were kept locked.

"So little brats like the ones you encountered yesterday don't let the animals loose. Or worse, enter the barn and get into mischief that can hurt themselves or the animals."

"Makes perfect sense," I murmured to myself, feeling slightly embarrassed at having asked the question.

"Here's a thought," went on Barbara. "Why not come with me tomorrow as I volunteered to take Mr. Hill's two calves, whose farm borders on our property, to the barn? You can get your usual walk in and be doing a good deed at the same time."

"Thank you for offering, I think I would enjoy that very much." I was beginning to have feelings for Barbara, and the vision of leisurely strolling next to her through the fields, calves in tow, made me smile.

She smiled in return.

I worked late that evening so that I could complete the rare book catalogue, and it was only when I was ready to retire to bed that I spotted Barbara's book on the shelf. Barbara must have shelved it incorrectly, as the volume certainly did not appear to be old. I took the book from the shelf and checked its publication date, which was just three years previous.

There was a bookmark near the middle, and I presumed this was the spot where Barbara had last read when I first entered the room. As the book had been returned to the shelf, I did not feel I would be betraying Barbara's privacy by flipping through its pages. I opened to the bookmarked page, revealing a poem by Walter de la Mare. A stanza was circled in pencil:

> *They told me Pan was dead, but I*
> *Oft marvelled who it was that sang*
> *Down the green valleys languidly*
> *Where the grey elder-thickets hang.*

On the opposite page was an image that unnerved me—that of the great god Pan, who had a bestial form, combining the physical features of both goat and man. His torso was that of a man, but he had the horns and ears of a goat, and hooves for feet. He was holding a panpipe, the double-reeded musical instrument bearing his name. The look upon his face was both playful yet mischievous. I thought it a horrid expression, and was glad when I shelved the book.

I did not have a peaceful sleep that night, a strange melody kept playing in my mind, like the one I fancied I heard earlier in the day. And certain phrases from Barbara's book also came to mind, especially those in the caption below Pan's image: *guardian of flocks and herds; symbol of bestial lust; inducer of panic terror.*

I awoke to a warm, sunny morning, and the thought of meeting Barbara lifted my spirits considerably after my restless night. When I entered the breakfast room, I was surprised to see both Richard and Lord Johnson at the table. Barbara introduced me to Lord Johnson, who appeared delighted to meet me, before she motioned for me to take the seat next to her.

"Barbara has told me how diligently you have been working day and night in order to complete the cataloguing of my rare books," Lord Johnson remarked. "I must thank the university for sending someone as capable as you."

"I've enjoyed the opportunity to look through such an impressive collection of rare volumes. You'll be pleased to know that I completed cataloguing them last night, and I can begin on the remaining shelves today."

Lord Johnson congratulated me on my progress and asked if I could leave my papers with Richard after breakfast. "Absolutely," I replied, "they are sitting on the side table next to the bay window."

"I'll get them later, Uncle," said Richard. "There's really no need to trouble yourself, William."

"As you please," I replied.

"But before William continues with his work," began Barbara, "he has volunteered to help me take Walter's calves to the barn this morning. I fancy our guest has taken a liking to country living," she teased.

"I admit, I've enjoyed taking in the fresh air and idyllic surrounding during my afternoon strolls, such a refreshing change from the noise and smog of the city."

"I'm glad to hear it," said Lord Johnson pleasantly. "Now off you go, the two of you. I shan't keep you chatting at the breakfast table any longer. I will see both of you at dinner."

Farmer Walter was waiting for us at the end of his drive with his two calves, each wearing a rope halter with a six-foot lead, which he handed to us. As with Lord Johnson, he seemed quite pleased to meet me. As we lead the calves to the barn by way of a meandering dirt lane, we encountered a few other farmers, all of whom shook my hand and greeted me cheerfully.

"Is everyone here so nice?" I inquired as we approached the barn.

"You're somewhat of a celebrity. It's not often we get a scholar visiting us." She handed me her lead as we stopped in front of the barn doors. "It's been very nice having you here," she added in a gentler tone.

"Barbara..." I hesitated briefly before continuing, "do you think... if it's alright with you, of course... that I could see you again after my travels?"

She took a step forward and placed her hand gently upon mine. "I would like that very much, William." I stood there silently for a few moments, savouring the delicate touch of her hand on mine, until she turned to remove the wooden bar that secured the doors before unlocking the padlock with a key she took from her pocket. Sliding open one of the doors, she said to me;

"I'll let you do the honours. Just remove their halters once inside and they'll start running around and playing in no time."

I led the calves a few feet into the barn, then did as Barbara said. The animals immediately headed towards the hay stacks scattered about the place. Sunlight streamed through the openings between the barn's wooden slats, illuminating the forward section of the barn, while the back remained in shadows. It suddenly seemed as if the darkness crept forward, but the effect was due to Barbara having shut the barn door behind me. I went over to it and was surprised when it refused to open.

"Barbara, the door is stuck, can you open it from your side. I don't relish the though of playing baby sitter to the calves all day."

There was no reply. I banged on the door several times with my fist and called out again, "Barbara—" I fell silent as I suddenly became aware of a plaintive flute melody originating from the rear of the barn. I turned slowly to find the two calves a few feet away, motionless, their gaze fixed towards the back of the barn. I called out, "Who's there? Is that you, Pam? You can come out, I won't hurt you," I added reassuringly. At that moment, the music stopped, and a low laughter echoed from one of the corners—a malevolent laughter, one that made my skin crawl—followed by the sudden stomping of a hoof.

Barbara stood silently outside the barn doors as the town folks gathered around her. The small crowd parted when Richard and Lord Johnson arrived, allowing them to take their place beside Barbara.

"Any moment now," she said to them.

There was a shriek of horror from within the barn, followed by the rattling of the doors as William tried frantically to exit the barn.

"Don't be afraid, William," Barbara whispered mockingly, "It's just our lovely flutist..."

There were several more cries for help, followed by another yell of dreadful terror.

"He sure is a loud one," commented Lord Johnson, "do you think Pan will like him as a playmate?"

"Oh yes," Barbara assured him, "he'll enjoy playing with a human for a change. It's been over a year since we presented him with one. And William is much younger and more handsome than the last fellow."

"How long do you think he will last?" asked Richard.

"As long as the others, I suspect," replied Barbara. "Two weeks at the most, after which his mind and body will fail him. Farmer Jack has already volunteered to dispose of the body as feed for his hogs."

"Very decent of the fellow," added Lord Johnson, "I must drop by later and thank him personally."

The gathering continued to wait patiently outside the barn until the haunting melody of a flute was heard, the sign that the great god Pan was pleased. The crowd slowly started to disperse, confident in the knowledge that it would be an excellent year for their farms.

SUMMER BLOOD

Muskoka Lakes, Canada, 1929

Darkness deepened rapidly on the densely wooded island as the sun disappeared beneath the horizon. An evening mist rose from the lake and slowly crept its way inland. As it encircled a large maple tree, the creature lying beneath the dense canopy opened its eyes and lifted itself from the damp ground. It was time to hunt, and what it yearned for most was the blood of humans.

The small, uninhabited island was not more than twenty minutes by rowboat from the mainland. It was a favourite getaway for lovers, who would stealthily row their boats to either of the two makeshift docks situated on opposite ends of the island. Several days of rain had deterred anyone from visiting, but the weather had finally improved that morning, leaving the water calm.

The creature lurked among the trees near the shoreline, patiently awaiting its prey. It could detect the breath of a human from more than one-hundred feet away, and it did not have to wait long before it caught the first hint of a woman's breath. It followed the stream of exhaled molecules towards the shoreline, all the while scanning its surroundings with its bulbous eyes, finely tuned to detect the heat emitted from a human body.

There! A couple strolling leisurely along the coastline. The woman was walking nearest to the woods, presenting an easy target. A quick strike to the neck would supply all the nourishment it required for several days. It would execute its attack with such stealth that neither human would have time to react to its presence.

It waited for the couple to walk by before it approached from behind, gliding noisily, its long, sharp, sucking organ now protruding grotesquely from its mouth. Ten feet distance...five feet...two...

"Ouch!" cried the woman, slapping the side of her neck with the palm of her hand. "A pesky mosquito just bit me!" she added with a voice of indignation.

Her companion chuckled heartily.

"My dear, I don't see why you take so much pleasure in my being bitten. There's nothing humorous about it."

My apologies...my...darling," he replied, trying his best to stifle his laughter. "But I could not help but see the irony of the situation: a vampire gets bitten in the neck by a mosquito!"

The woman's face softened as she looked at her husband lovingly, a widening smile revealing her white fangs, gleaming in the rays of the moonlight.

"I must admit, my love, there is a humorous element to the situation."

"Why of course there is, my precious. I would never—"

"Shush!" interrupted the women in a low tone, reaching out suddenly to touch his arm. "Look there," she whispered, pointing to a clump of pine trees on the opposite bank. He followed the direction of her finger to a spot where the occasional flickering of a light could be seen.

"A campfire," uttered the husband with delight. He raised his head and sniffed the air. "There are two of them, in the prime of their youth." He turned to his wife and took her by the hands, a smile broadening across his face. "My love," he said with excitement in his voice, "this is going to be a wonderful evening."

She kissed him gently upon the lips, then took his arm as he proudly led her towards a feast of summer blood.

EXCERPT FROM A
TAROT PROPHESY

Captured Souls (English
Lake District, 1858)

Lewis set the bouquet of Daffodils on her grave. Her tombstone lay towards the back of the churchyard, next to the old stone wall that enclosed the small cemetery of St. Bede. Engraved at the top of the tombstone were two hands clasped together—a testament to their everlasting love. Below the engraving, the epitaph read: *Harriet Parker. Her light will shine eternally. Requiescat In Pace.*

"Rest in peace, my love," he said tenderly, "When the time comes, we will walk hand-in-hand once more, as we used to."

It was just a few months ago that they had settled in the village of Elterwater, where he found employment as a bookkeeper at the gunpowder plant. Harriet was delighted when he told her the news. She loved the countryside and was eager to leave the crowded streets of London behind to begin a new life in Elterwater with him. They took up residence in a cozy cottage by a gentle stream, one of the many waterways that fed into the main river powering the factory. While he was away at work, she roamed the region in search of inspiration for her artwork, a series of landscape paintings commissioned by a dear friend of hers. It was during one of these outings that she came to discover the church at St. Bede.

The small church stood alone in a meadow along the western edge of the lake, two tall elm trees flanking the low stone wall surrounding both the church and its cemetery. A small wooden gate facing the rear of the church provided the only entrance into the church grounds. On the opposite shore of the lake, a series of imposing, craggy peaks towered above, dwarfing the church in comparison.

Beautiful beyond words, thought Harriet as she absorbed the subtle details of the scenery that lay before her, *this will be an absolute joy to paint.*

She went there almost every day, with her easel and pochade box in tow, painting the church and its surroundings for hours on end. On a singularly hot and humid afternoon, as Harriet was putting the final touches to her painting, a great thunderstorm caught her by surprise, forcing her to seek shelter under the canopy of one of the great elm trees. "Of all the rotten luck," she said out loud, as a clap of thunder broke overhead and a sudden gust of wind swayed the towering branches above her.

That evening Lewis arrived home to find a clergyman waiting for him outside his cottage gate.

"Reverend Anderson, what brings you here?" He glanced past the reverend to the closed door of the cottage. "Has Harriet not yet returned?"

Clearing his throat, the reverend replied in a subdued voice, "As you are probably aware, there was a violent storm this afternoon. Mrs. Parker was caught unawares and took shelter under an elm tree by the church yard. One of its large boughs broke free by the fierce wind, badly injuring your wife. By the time I found her, there was little I could do to save her. I'm so sorry, Mr. Parker."

Lewis stood in silence, then the meaning of the reverend's words took hold and he felt sick, his head spinning and his legs ready to give way. He swallowed hard and said unsteadily, "My...Harriet..."

The reverend nodded slowly. "You can take some solace in knowing that I had time to administer her last rights, Mr. Parker. Before her parting, she asked that I convey her final words to you—that she loves you, and that she wishes to be buried at St. Bede's cemetery. She passed away peacefully soon after communicating this to me."

Suddenly, the reverend reached out and caught Lewis by the arms before gently laying him down on the ground. The poor fellow had fainted.

Her tombstone cast its long shadow in the waning daylight. "It's time for me to go, Harriet, but I'll be back soon." He was about to leave but after a moment's reflection spoke to her once more. "By the way, I almost forgot to tell you, there are some lovely forget-me-nots growing next to the hedgerows we planted, a vibrant azure colour. I'll collect a bunch and bring them with me tomorrow. They will complement the daffodils quite nicely."

Reaching out, he placed his hand on her tombstone. He held it there for a minute before turning away and slowly heading towards the gate. This was the most difficult part of the day, leaving her all alone in the small graveyard. *Just ten minutes more,* he muttered to himself. *I can't face the thought of going back to an empty house just yet.*

He wandered among the tombstones, noting that most appeared quite old, the headstones stained green with the encroachment of moss over time. He read some of the dates as he walked past. *Seventeen-eighty-nine, seventeen—*

He suddenly paused and focused his attention on the epitaph beneath the date. Most of the words were too worn down to be read, while others were encrusted with fungal growth. But a few letters stood out clearly, as if recently scrubbed clean.

"H-e-l-p" he murmured. Below these, two more letters were visible; "m-e."

"Help me," he said in bewilderment. "How very queer." He scanned the epitaph carefully once more, but those were the sole decipherable letters. Hesitantly, he walked up to the tombstone. The engraving at the top featured a bible. *This must be a grave of a minister,* he thought. He tried to decipher the name. The first few letters read 'Brad'. He used his nail to scrape away at the dried moss that covered the remainder of the name. Small flakes of green fell away revealing the letters 'dock'.

"Braddock," he said in a slow, puzzled voice. "I'll ask Reverend Anderson about the name, perhaps Braddock was a clergyman at St. Bede. Uncanny about the message, though. Just a rare fluke I suppose, such events must occur sometimes. Still...I can't shake the feeling that there is something to this. Perhaps—"

He broke his train of thought to look up towards the gate. Darkness had settled in, and a sudden feeling of unease fell upon him as he fixed his gaze at what looked like the silhouette of a man.

"Reverend Anderson?" Lewis asked in a lowered voice.

There was no reply as the shadowy figure faded into the darkness.

ALSO BY STEPHEN TALLEVI

A Tarot Prophecy and Other Stories

"A must-read for horror enthusiasts" - Literary Titan.

"A darkly wonderful anthology of horror short stories. The author is a master of the short horror story." - Readers View

"An exceptional and must-read collection." - Book Nerdection

The Inheritance and Other Dark Tales

"*The Inheritance and Other Dark Tales is not for the faint of heart...a thrilling read for fans of horror*"
– Readers' Favorite

" *A gripping collection of horror stories...a brilliant and unforgettable book.*" - Literary Titan

A native of Ontario, Canada, Stephen intertwines his academic prowess with a lifelong passion for the paranormal. Growing up with tales of "true" ghost stories from his grandparents' séances and after-school sessions with "The Twilight Zone", Stephen has cultivated a deep-seated fascination for stories that delve into the dark and paranormal genres. Stephen brings a unique blend of scholarly insight and personal intrigue to his writing, creating tales that not only entertain but also resonate with a chilling touch of authenticity.